Unsound Mind

A.J. Montana

ISBN: 978-1-7384935-1-7

Cover design by: Rachel Coulson
Map created in Inkarnate

I'd like to say a massive thank you to Matthew, Christine, Kelly and Meg for taking the time to read Unsound Mind prior to its release.

Also, a huge thank you to Rachel for designing the cover.

Without all of you, this book would still be a work in progress.

Chapter One

No one knows to this day what happened in there

Camera, check. Wallet, check. Now, where are my keys? I mulled, zipping the black duffle bag I had packed; it sat on the end of the bed next to my dark brown leather jacket. I then blindly searched the awful silk duvet, but it was too dark to make anything out. I also didn't want to wake my wife, who was sleeping soundly.

A sigh escaped me as I glimpsed over her. *God, I don't know how we'll manage in five months...* Shaking off that thought, I turned for the oak dresser. It was pressed against the usually stark white wall facing the bed, the bedroom door just to the right. *Where are they?* I wondered, brushing a hand along the top of the dresser before frustration started to seep in. *Fuck it, I'm gonna be late!*

Deciding to check the nightstand on my side of the bed, I rushed past the white blinds along the back wall that overlooked a bustling street, making them rattle. *Shit!* The noise stirred my wife; I didn't dare move until I heard little purr-like snores again. Expelling a heavy breath, I checked the nightstand, but my keys were still nowhere to be found. *Fuck it!*

Scrubbing a hand through my dishevelled brown hair, I decided to check the living-room next, so I crept back around and snatched the bag, slinging it over my shoulder. Lastly, I grabbed my leather jacket before the sound of metal hit the hardwood floor with a ding. *Shit!* I cursed again, glancing down to see my keys had landed by my black and white, hi-top converses; my dark grey jeans were haphazardly tucked into them.

Then the rustle of sheets gained my attention; I peered over to see my wife half propped up.

"Travis?" She groggily wondered, squinting at the clock on her nightstand, "It's five in the morning... What are you doing up so early?"

Picking up my keys, I explained, "I need to leave now if I'm gonna get back in time to pick the kids up from school. But if I'm running late, I'll give Hayleigh a call."

"Before you go," She began, switching on the lamp that momentarily blinded me, "Did your nan send you those photos?"

"Ahhh, fuck..." I groaned, bringing a hand up to pinch the bridge of my nose, "I forgot to ask..."

"Oliver needs them for school tomorrow!" She heatedly growled.

I lowered my hand to see her glowering, her green eyes blazing in frustration.

"Harper, calm down." I spoke softly, trying not to lose my temper, "I'll call her and get her to send them to our e-mail."

"Make sure you do." She retorted while sitting up, her light blue vest partially hidden by her long, startling blonde hair; it tumbled down her pale, slender shoulders in waves.

A tightness formed in my jaw as I stared at her in irritation. *What else does she want me to say?! I already told her I'd do it!*

Choosing not to voice my thoughts out loud, I planted a quick kiss on Harper's cheek, saying, "Keep me updated today, okay? And remember, no peeking until I'm home."

A slight mischievous grin crept along her lips, "I'm not promising anything."

"Don't even think about it." I firmly retorted, but I couldn't stop a small smile from pulling at the corners of my mouth. Turning for the bedroom door, I said, "I'll see you later. And remember, get some sleep."

My shoes squeaked against the hardwood floor when I stepped into the white-walled hallway, carefully closing the door behind me just as the pungent odour of greasy food smacked me in the face. We lived in a flat directly above a kebab shop; the only rooms that didn't strongly reek were the two bedrooms and the open plan living-room as they had windows, which overlooked the high street.

Making sure to be quiet when I passed the children's room on my left, I headed straight to the front door just down the hallway on the right. *Urrgh, it's getting worse...* I retched when I opened it and was greeted by the stale smell of piss. Once I had somewhat regained myself, I hurried down the stairwell and practically kicked open the door, coming to stand outside the kebab shop called Abra-Kebabra. *Argggh, I can't ever get away from that fucking smell!* Even outside, I could still smell the greasiness that, somehow, lingered in the atmosphere.

A chillness hung in the September air, so I swiftly pulled on my jacket, hiding my burnt orange t-shirt from view. I then readjusted my duffle bag before leaving, going to my car in the designated parking outside the row of shops.

I better call JJ. I pondered, twirling my keys around my index finger. *Just to make sure he's awak-*

"You've got to be fucking kidding me!" I growled, spotting a bright yellow piece of paper pinned under the window wiper. *Why the fuck have I got a ticket?!* Ripping it free, I immediately opened it. *What the?!* '**Vehicle has no valid Parking Permit**' was ticked. *But I do have a perm- Oh for fuck's sake...* I groaned aloud when I noticed my permit had been replaced with a pink piece of paper; '**DaDDy's ParkiNg PurrmiT**' was scrawled across it in my five-year-old son's handwriting.

I can't fucking afford this! I seethed, fisting the ticket in question before unlocking my car; it was an old, beaten-up, red Nissan Micra which I absolutely detested. *I really need to start looking for something bigger, but I just can't afford it...* Emitting a heavy breath, I clambered in the driver's side, tossing the duffle bag into the back. I then stuffed the ticket into the glovebox and would probably forget about it.

Right, better phone JJ. I reminded, allowing myself to relax momentarily as I slumped into the surprisingly comfy grey seats, mindlessly fiddling with my silver wedding band. I then retrieved my Nokia from my jacket pocket, tapping through the contacts until I found JJ. Pressing the green button, I propped the phone against my ear while clipping in my seatbelt, uncertain whether he would answer as it kept ringing and ringing. *Come on. Pick up... Pick up!*

Just as I was about to pull away, a groggy voice answered, "Hello?"

"I'll be about forty-odd minutes." I bluntly said, glimpsing at the driver's side mirror before setting off.

"Hi, Josh, how are you?" JJ mimicked my gruff voice before carrying on in his usual upbeat tone, "A tad tired but can't complain. How are you, bud?" Then he imitated my voice again, "A dick like always."

"Har har har..." I grumbled, adjusting the phone so I was now holding it with my right hand, "You're sooooo fucking funny..."

"Jooooooosh, come back to bed!" JJ's girlfriend, Allison, groaned in the background.

Ignoring her, he replied, "Of course I'm funny, one of us gotta be!"

"Josh!" Allison abruptly scolded, but JJ wasn't swayed and said to me, "If you're on your way, I better get going. I'll see you soon, bud."

He hung up before I got the chance to respond.

The quietness that now lingered in the car allowed my mind to mull over all my worries. I couldn't help but bite my bottom lip, reaching for my emergency pack of cigarettes in the glovebox once I had discarded my phone on the passenger seat. Using my mouth to pull out a cigarette, I tossed the packet beside my mobile while fretting. *What will I do if this story is a flop as well? I'll be without a job for a start!* I then rummaged inside my jacket pocket, finding a lighter. *Then what? Retail? Hospitality? I hate that shit!*

Lighting the cigarette, I took a massive pull and expelled the puff of noxious smoke, relaxing before all my worries crashed over me again. *I need a distraction!* Discarding the lighter next to my phone, I turned on the radio.

"And in at number twenty-two is '**Sleeping With The Light On**', which has dropped by fourteen since last week!" The male radio host announced, and I couldn't help but inwardly groan.

Not this fucking song again... I wasn't a fan of Busted, but my three-year-old daughter was, so I had endured my fair share.

"Stay tuned for more official top chart singles." The radio host carried on, and I could hear the beginning of the song

by the strum of a guitar.
"For all of those who have just tuned in, it's Monday 8th September, and you're listening to the official top chart singles for 2003!"

'**Along sheee caaaaame, with heeer piiictuuure. Put it in aaaa fraaame, so III woooon't miss heer. Got on aaaa plaaane, from London; Heeathrooow. It seems suuuch a shaaaame, yeeaah... I FEEL HEEER, SLIP-**'. I had heard enough, so I quickly changed the station.

"A thirty-year-old man from Salemburg has been reported missing whilst on his brother's stag do in July earlier this year." A female news reporter chimed in, and I couldn't help but wonder why it was being made public two months later. *He's probably dead...* I deliberated, deciding to put in my mix tape.

I tried to immerse myself in the music for the rest of the journey but was too anxious about work. *What if this story is just utter shit?* My stomach churned at that notion, so I shifted in my seat but could not get comfortable. *How the fuck are we gonna afford things if this story doesn't pan out? Craig's gonna let me go if I fuck up again...*

I soon pulled up outside JJ's house; it was along a quaint little street, which had surprised me when I had first met him as he never struck me as the white picket fence kind of guy. *I think he's too proud to admit his parents have helped him...* I couldn't deny that I envied him, but I also knew his parents could only express love and affection through money. *I'd much rather be poor and have a family than this façade shit he's got going on.*

Scrubbing a hand through my hair, a growl seeped from my lips when a few slithers fell into my eyes. *I really need to get a haircut...* I muttered, glancing at my reflection in the rear-view mirror, noting how tired I looked; dark circles matched my dark brown eyes. *Well... I look as shit as I feel...* It didn't help I hadn't had time to shave this morning; a fine layer of dark stubble adorned my sculpted jaw. *At least it's hiding those awful acne scars...* They had faded as I got older, so they were hardly noticeable, but I always knew they were there.

Just as I finished setting up the map and moved my stuff off the passenger seat, light pooled down the garden path, distracting me. JJ appeared with a bag slung over his shoulder, seemingly clad in one of those awful tracksuits teenagers would wear. It was strange as I was used to seeing him dressed to the nines in a designer suit that emphasised his lean, muscle-bound body. *Why the hell is he wearing that?...* But I shook off that deliberation, watching as he waved goodbye to Allison before trudging down the path as if the weight of the world was bearing down on him.

"What's up with you?" I asked as soon as JJ hopped in the car, stuffing the bag between his feet.
His trainers were such a startling white; I could only guess they were brand-new.

"Urgh..." He groaned, momentarily shaking his head.
His coiffed, dark brown hair was liberally gelled, so much so it didn't move.
"Just money worries..." He murmured, and I couldn't help but scoff, "Money worries?"

I waited for JJ to buckle in before driving off.
"What about your parents?" I pondered, "Aren't they gonna help?"
Part of me hoped – *No, prayed* – that he finally understood what it meant to have no money.

"Of course they're going to help!" He replied with a laugh, as if the idea of them not was ludicrous, "But I've still had to make cutbacks, like where we shop and what we eat."

"You poor thing..." I uttered, knowing his cutbacks were not on the same level as mine.

"Is that a hint of sarcasm I detect there, bud?" JJ queried; I immediately shot him a '**I don't know what you're talking about**' look when his green eyes locked on me.
"Sarcasm aside," He continued when I didn't reply, burying his left hand inside his light grey tracksuit pocket; I could just see his Japanese sleeve tattoo peek out the cuff.
"I can't be back late tonight. It's mine and Ali's three-year anniversary." He then pulled out a packet of cigarettes.

"Yeah, I can't be back late either." I agreed, shaking my head when he offered me one.
I should really stop... I deliberated, watching him pop a cigarette into his mouth. *I will have to soon, anyway. I can't afford to keep buying them...* That thought had me divert my attention back to the road just as he lit it.

"I've got to pick the kids up from school as Harper's got a hospital appointment." I explained.
JJ lowered the cigarette, a look of concern gracing his chiselled face.
"Everything okay?" He wondered, rolling down the window a crack.
Do I tell him? I mulled but then shook my head at that idea. *We've not told anyone else yet…* Then the reality of the situation came crashing over me. *We already struggle as it is without throwing a baby into the mix… Please,* ***please*** *may this story be a success!*
"Travis?" JJ piped up, gaining my attention as he blew a puff of smoke out the window, "Everything okay with Harper?"
I nodded once, not ready to tell him about her pregnancy.
"Fine…" I murmured, fixing my attention back on the road, "Everything's fine…"
I knew he wasn't convinced; I felt his eyes practically burn a hole right through me, so I swiftly tacked on, "I just can't fuck this up, okay? Craig said this is our last chance after all the cock ups." That comment made him snicker.
What the hell's he laughing about?
"That story you covered last week was pure gold!" JJ enthusiastically exclaimed, "'**Homicide victims won't talk to police.**'!" He then burst into a fit of hysterical laughter.
Fuck you! I inwardly growled, grinding my teeth as a deterrent not to snap.
"Well, you can't exactly talk, can you?" I retorted, and JJ abruptly went silent as I continued mockingly, "'**Teen pregnancy statistics drastically drop after the age of twenty.**'… '**Russia uses sea to hide its submarines.**'… I could go on."
"Don't, just don't…" He grumbled before flicking his cigarette out the window, grabbing another and lighting it.
When JJ started playing with his mobile, it reminded me I needed to phone my nan.
"What's the time?" I queried, and he replied, "Half six, why?"
"I've just got to make a quick call."
"Isn't it a bit early to be calling someone?" He asked with a furrowed brow, and I shook my head, "My nan's usually up at the crack of dawn. Doesn't want to waste daylight hours or what not…"

JJ's eyes lit up at the mention of my nan, "How is Nanna Moon?"
"Fine, I guess." I flatly responded, unsure why he always asked about her when they had never met.

I then grabbed my Nokia from the centre console, my attention constantly flitting between the road and my contacts as I tapped through. When I eventually found my nan, I pressed the green button and propped the phone against my ear with my shoulder.

After several rings, my nan's whisper of a voice answered, "Hello?"

I couldn't help but smile as I said, "Hey, Nan, it's just me."

I had a soft spot for my nan and would move heaven and earth for her. After all, she had raised me once my parents got divorced. *I never saw my dad after that, and my mum moved on with another guy...* Not that I could remember them; I was only two at the time. *I think Nan liked the company after losing Grandad.* I had never met him; he went missing a few months after I was born. *They never did find out what happened...*

"Ruh-Rick?" My nan queried tremulously; I couldn't help but inwardly groan as it had been a reoccurring incident for the past year.

Funny at first, but now it's starting to get irritating... Our telephone calls would all start the same. *Her thinking I'm Grandad...*

"No, it's Travis." I corrected, sighing in frustration when my nan replied, "Travis isn't here. Would you like me to take a message?"

"No, Nan, **I'M** Travis!" I snapped a little too readily; all the while, JJ was snickering.

"Travis?!" She gawked, as if it finally sunk in, "Don't you dare raise your voice at me, young man!"

Guilt instantly consumed me; I knew it wasn't her fault, what with being partially deaf and dementia setting in, but it still didn't change how incredibly frustrating it was.

"I'm sorry, Nan-" I began, but she swiftly cut across, "Back in my day, my father would've given me a good seeing to if I raised my voice at him!"

"I know, Nan, and I'm sorr-"

"You youngsters nowadays get away with murders!" She continued; I tried to get a word in edgeways, but she was lost in her tangent, "I don't know why such a big hoo-ha was made about hitting children. If you want my opinion, there's nothing wrong with a smack to put them on the straight and narrow."

"Anyway!" I declared when my nan paused for a breather, "I'm calling to ask if you can send those family photos over, along with the names if you can remember them."

"Oh, crumbs!" She grumbled; I could vividly envision her shaking her head.

"I'm sorry, pet, I completely forgot. If you pop round this weekend, we can sort-"

"I need them today." I explained, adjusting my mobile so I held it with my right hand, "Oliver needs them for school tomorrow."

"Okay, give me one tick, and I'll turn my laptop on."

The thud of the phone being set down echoed in my ear. I could hear her shuffling around, murmuring to herself. A good ten minutes passed before she finally returned.

"Okay, I've turned the laptop on. What do I do now?" My nan queried, so I explained, "I need you to go onto your e-mail and-"

"Is that the '**e**' icon?" She interrupted.

I found it hard not to lose my patience as I spoke through gritted teeth, "That's the internet, which you do need to go on to access your e-mail."

"So, I press it?" She asked.

I then talked her through step-by-step what she needed to do, reiterating to send the photos to mine and Harper's e-mail. A sigh of relief escaped me once she confirmed she had sent them.

"Thanks again, Nan." I breathed, slumping back in the seat as all the tension seeped from me, "But I've got to go now. We'll come and see you on the weekend, okay?"

"That would be lovely, pet. I'll give you a bell Friday evening."

"Perfect, I'll speak to you then. Love you."

"Love you too, pet."

Once I discarded my Nokia in the centre console, JJ abruptly exclaimed, "My! Fucking! God! When you said you needed to make a quick call, I didn't expect you to be on the phone for over half a fucking hour!"

"Yeah, well, I didn't think I'd be that long either..." I uttered as he flicked a cigarette out the window, pulling out another; it was only then it dawned on me how much he smoked.

Speaking through the cigarette as he lit it, JJ queried, "Any chance we can stop along the way, bud?"

I automatically peered over at the map strewn across the dashboard before shaking my head, "No, we'll be there in less than an hour."

He glanced at it before doing a doubletake, noticing the circled area, "We've got miles to go, Travis!" He griped, "I need a coffee or something!"

"I thought you couldn't be back late?" I countered, and he opened his mouth to argue but clearly thought better of it.

Once he had stopped quietly stewing, JJ changed the subject, "Where are we going, anyway? You haven't told me anything about this story we're covering."

How do I explain it to him?

Scrubbing a hand across my jaw, I began, "A mental asylum. We're going to a mental asylum."

I didn't need to look at him to know he was staring at me in disbelief.

"A mental asylum?" JJ repeated, "They're, what? Just letting us in to talk to the patients?"

Shaking my head, I stated, "It's abandone-"

"Hell! Fucking! No!" He intervened, frantically shaking his head, "I'm not going into some haunted nut hut!"

Gesturing with my hand for him to calm down, I urged, "Just hear me out! Twenty-six years ago, the asylum was put into lockdown by a Doctor Sasin. All the nurses, doctors, and all that were locked inside with the patients. No one knows to this day what happened in there."

"Then how do **you** know all this?" JJ retorted, so I explained further, "No one was answering the door to visitors... The phones weren't being picked up... Family of staff hadn't seen or heard from them in days... So the police broke in but never publicly announced what they found. After the investigation, they boarded up all the doors and windows."

"And no one else has thought to break in, which I presume we're doing?..." JJ uttered, clearly unconvinced.

"Of course other people have." I confirmed.

He then held up a hand, gesturing for me to wait while questioning, "Let me guess, they all went missing?"

I couldn't help but laugh, "No!" I then regained myself before carrying on, "They went mad. Cut their tongues out so they could never share their story."

"Riiiiiight..." He sceptically murmured, flicking his cigarette out the window before grabbing another, "Sure..."

***

"Where the fuck are we going, Travis?!" JJ griped, fisting his empty packet of cigarettes and tossing it down into the footwell. I couldn't help but eye the other two boxes littered by his feet, the car lingering with stale cigarette fumes. *I don't fucking know!* I bristled, drumming my fingers along the steering wheel to release some pent-up energy. Struggling to keep my rapidly growing anger at bay, I peered around the once picturesque street we were driving down. The white picket fences were weathered, the gardens overgrown and hiding the windows from view. *Where's the asylum?*

"We've been driving around for an hour!" JJ heatedly carried on before waving a hand, correcting himself, "No, wait, **two** fucking hours!" He held up his middle and index fingers, "Do you even know where the hell we are?!"

If I knew where we were, I wouldn't be driving around in fucking circles! With forced restraint, I remained silent once more, but I could feel my patience wear thin by his barrage of questions.

"You know I can't be home late!" JJ fumed; I couldn't stop my teeth from grinding when he kept going on, "You might not care about your relationship and keeping your wife happy, but this day is special to me and-"

"Just shut the fuck up!" I snapped, unable to listen to his whining a moment longer, "I'm not purposely driving around to piss you off! It's not my fucking fault this area isn't on the fucking map!" A shiver crept up my spine when those words left my lips.

Memories of us reaching the circled area on the map flooded my mind; it was a forest thick with fog and not the mental asylum. I still couldn't quite put my finger on what had given me such chills, as if someone had walked over my grave. At first, I presumed it was the crumbling, sixty-foot wall we drove through; it once surrounded the forest and the now abandoned town we were driving aimlessly around. But there was something about the forest itself as if it were hiding a deep, dark secret amidst its impenetrable fog.

Shaking off my unease, I angrily added, "And it doesn't help everything looks the fucking same!"

I gestured around at the Stepford-looking houses before sharply turning right at the end of the road.

"If I knew where the Goddamn asylum was, do you think I'd-"

The iconic Nokia tune cut across me.

Peering down at my mobile in the centre console, I spotted Harper's name. *Fuck, is something wrong?!* My thoughts went straight to the kids; I couldn't shake this fresh feeling of nerves, as if something terrible had happened. But then I began to fret about Harper and the baby.

Snatching my phone, I answered in a blind panic, "You okay?! What's wrong?!"

"Erm, nothing's wrong." Harper replied, the palpitations in my chest slowly easing as she continued, "I'm just phoning to ask if you've spoken to your nan about those photos."

Hasn't she checked her e-mail?...

"Nan said she sent them." I stated with a furrowed brow.

"Well, I've not had anything, and I need to print them off today." She replied, making a heavy sigh escape me.

"Fuck it..." I cursed under my breath, propping the mobile against my shoulder so I could scrape my fingers through my hair.

What e-mail did she send them to?

"Travis? Are you there?" Harper piped up when I didn't respond; I didn't know what to say.

I thought I got it all sorted... One less thing to worry about...

"I'll check my e-mails when I pull over and let you know." I sighed, and there was a moment of silence before Harper pried, "Aren't you there yet?"

I didn't get the chance to clarify as she shot question after question at me.

"I thought you said you would be there by seven? Where are you then? And what about my hospital appointment? Are you even going to be back in time to pick Oliver and Hannah up?"

When I finally got the opportunity to speak, JJ nudged my arm, gaining my attention. He pointed at a direction sign with Merriwell Sanatorium faded into it, so I followed.

"Well?!" Harper urged, dragging me back to the conversation.
Adjusting the mobile so it was now in my right hand, I replied, "I got a little lost, but we've just made it. Let me park up, and I'll check my e-mail."

"Okay, but please be quick as I've got to go out."

As soon as I had said goodbye to Harper, I realised we were no longer in the suburban town; countryside now stretched as far as the eye could see. *Where are we? And where's this asylum?* Then I spotted a splintered wooden sign along the verge on my left, partially hidden amongst the overgrown shrubbery. Merriwell Sanatorium was carved into it in a large, cursive font.

"There it is!" JJ proclaimed, nudging me once more whilst enthusiastically pointing to the sign.

"Yeah, yeah, I see it." I acknowledged, slowing down just in time to notice a concealed entrance.

"What are you doing?!" He gaped when I turned onto the dilapidated gravel track, the car bottoming out when it hit a pothole.
"It's too narrow!" He warned and, as if on cue, twigs and leaves dragged along the car from overgrown bushes and overhanging trees with a screech.

When the lane finally opened up and revealed a rusty security gate, JJ wondered, "Why didn't you just park along the verge?" But I ignored him, more concerned with how we would get over the gate and into the asylum.
We can't even climb over the wall... I mulled, peering at the brick wall, which had clearly seen better days. It was attached to the gate with barbwire coiled along the top.

A heavy sigh then distracted me. I glimpsed at JJ, who was rummaging inside his bag, pulling out another packet of cigarettes.
"Well, this was a waste of time..." He uttered through gritted teeth.

"Then why did you fucking come?!" I snapped, ripping the pack out of his grasp.

"Because I'm in the same boat as you! About to lose my job if I don't pull my finger out!"

I laughed at his pathetic excuse as he would never be in the same sinking boat I was.

"What's so funny?" JJ heatedly retorted.
Fisting the packet of cigarettes, I gutturally roared, "You'll **never** be in the same fucking boat as me!"
I tossed the pack at his chest before reaching into the back of the car, grabbing my bag.

"Go and look for a way in while I sort this photo bollocks out." I stridently ordered, ignoring his stunned face as I pulled out my laptop.
"Go on. Fuck off." I then began searching for the dongle in one of the side pockets.
Once he had somewhat regained himself, JJ grumbled, "Whatever..." He then swung open the door, not bothering to close it, before storming off toward the gate.

Shaking my head, I fitted the dongle and turned on the laptop, logging straight into my e-mail. There were a couple of messages from work I had ignored over the weekend, all of which emphasised that I would be jobless if the story wasn't a success. *It will be a success. It **will** be a success!* I positively chanted, marking them as unread.

I then scanned the rest of my inbox, praying my nan had sent the photos to the correct address and Harper had just overlooked it. However, a frustrated sigh seeped from my lips when I found the e-mail. *Why did she send it to mine when I told her to send it to our-*

BANG! I glimpsed out the window to my right, seeing JJ standing there with his hands pressed against the glass. A massive smile plagued his chiselled face, but it instantly dropped when he didn't get the desired reaction.

"Didn't that scare you?" He asked, pushing himself off the window and trudging to the passenger's side.

"Not really, no." I commented, opening the e-mail to make sure my nan had actually attached the photos, relieved to see she had.

"So, I found a way to get in." JJ announced as I scrolled through the photos, holding my head in my hands when I noticed she hadn't included any names.
For fuck's sake, Nan...
"What's up, bud?" He probed.
I peeked at him between my fingers and saw him glancing at the photos.

Lowering my hands, I replied frustratedly, "My nan sent the photos but didn't include the names."

"But they're your relatives..." He pointed out, tilting his head to one side in confusion, "Don't you know their names?"

"Not all their names." I countered, but he ignored me and wondered, "Whoa, who's the dude who looks like you?!"

What?

Glancing back at the highlighted family photo, I had no idea who he was talking about.

"Who?" I pondered, and JJ exclaimed in disbelief, "You're joking, right?! He's the spitting image of you!" He pointed at the man in question.

"No, he isn't!" I insisted, staring hard at the photo taken in a very 50's looking living-room.

I instantly recognised my nan as she still had the same rosy-cheeked smile. She was sat on a sofa with a toddler on her lap, who was much more interested in his toy car than smiling for the camera. *I'm guessing that's Dad...* Sat next to my nan was the man JJ was adamant I looked exactly like. I didn't recognise him, yet there was something familiar about him that I couldn't quite put my finger on.

"Who is he?" JJ pried, snapping me back to the conversation.

Shrugging, I shook my head, "I... I don't know... Maybe my grandad, but I've never seen a photo of him."

I stared at the photo for a moment longer before forwarding the e-mail to Harper.

"Anyway," I murmured, closing the laptop and stuffing it inside the bag, "You said you found a way to get over the gate?"

"Part of the wall has crumbled away, so we can squeeze through." JJ said, retrieving a camera and torch from his bag still tucked in the footwell.

Tossing mine into the back, I sighed, "Come on then, let's get this shit over and done with if we want to get home on time."

If the doors and windows are boarded up, how will we get in? I mulled as JJ led the way. *One must be broken if other people have managed before.*

"So, what's the story behind this place then?" JJ questioned as we sidled through the thick undergrowth, distracting me from my ponderings.

"It was used as a rehabilitation centre back in the 50's." I began, raising my arms above the twigs and thorns that snagged at my clothes, "Apparently, the whole town was drugged or something by the government."

"What do you mean drugged?" He sceptically probed, glancing over his shoulder at me when I replied, "Drugged as in drug drugged, like some kind of brainwashing medication."

"Hmmm..." He murmured in uncertainty, and I could honestly see how it was hard to believe.

Choosing to clarify what I understood of the situation, I carried on, "I think the government did it as some kind of experiment to see if there was an increase in productivity. But the doctors here at the asylum used different kinds of treatment to keep their patients doped up if they were found to no longer be taking it."

"Wow, talk about control freaks..." JJ muttered before coming to a halt by the collapsed part of the wall.

"So, was this Doctor Sasin guy you mentioned earlier part of the whole drug ordeal?" He wondered.

I shook my head, "No, he was brought in when the experiment was finally pulled. The asylum was then used to try and help the people become functioning members of society."

"Ha! I like the fact you said '**try**'..." He laughed once, yet there was no humour underlying his tone.

Gesturing with a sweep of his hand towards the gap in the wall, JJ offered with a one-sided smirk, "After you, my Liege."

I merely stared at him with daggers for a few moments before ducking down, squeezing through the tight gap where the barbwire snagged my hair.

Once I had freed myself and edged around the overgrown bushes, I came to stand in a garden that I imagined would have looked scenic in its heyday. Now it was overrun with weeds, the grass coming past my knees. Then my eyes locked onto the asylum, the gravel track serpentining from the gate all the way up to the entrance.

Whoa! I gaped, blown away by its sheer magnificence. *It's like something out of Harry Potter!* The baronial building, with its intricate rooflines decorated with cone-shaped roofs, small turrets, and crenelated walls with battlements, didn't fit in with what I had seen of the town. *Maybe that's why it's on the outskirts... Out of sight, out of mind kind of thing...*

"Well, that's fucking massive!" JJ piped up from behind me, and it was only now I became acutely aware of just how big the asylum was.
Buildings that looked like gothic terraced houses were linked to the main entrance on either side, stretching a daunting distance. Both ends appeared to have another baronial-looking facility attached, much smaller than the entrance block.

The click of a camera then gained my attention. I peered beside me to see JJ taking snaps of the asylum. *There's no way we'll be able to check all this today...* I mulled, glancing back at the building just as a wave of anxiety crashed over me. *What the fuck was I thinking?!* I worried, repeatedly rubbing my face. *This isn't gonna work! We're not gonna have a fucking story at this rate!*

"Travis?" JJ spoke up; I lowered my hand to see him staring at me sympathetically, "Shall we head on inside?"
Sighing, I nodded once, "Yeah, let's try the front door first, but I doubt it'll be unlocked."

We then made our way up the gravel driveway, our shoes crunching underfoot. As we drew nearer, I could see the tall, narrow, barred windows on the ivy-infested entrance block were boarded up. *Whoever broke in before didn't use the main entrance...* I murmured, vaguely aware of JJ taking a few more photos, so I advanced on the dark wood door with a ruined stone arch. I hoped it was unlocked, desperately needing some luck to keep me going.

After trying the knob several times and barging into the door with my shoulder, I just wanted to scream in frustration when it didn't budge.
"Fuck it!" I cursed under my breath with a shake of my head.
"No luck?" JJ queried as I turned to face him, shaking my head again.
How did other people get inside? I wondered, glimpsing back over at the windows. I could only presume they had somehow managed to bend the bars and remove the board. *But how-*

"Oh well." JJ abruptly commented with a shrug, "Guess we won't be going inside after all."
I got the distinct impression he was more than thrilled.
"What's that supposed to mean?" I queried with a furrowed brow.

"It means we tried, and that's that." He admitted, placing a consoling hand on my shoulder.
"Look, Travis, the windows are boarded up, and the door is locked. We **can't** get in." He quickly added when I opened my mouth to retort.
So, he's just giving up before we've even tried?

Despite the painfully obvious answer, I questioned, "You're giving up already when all we've done is try the front fucking door?!"

"It's not the end of the world." JJ reassured me; his comment made my hands clench into fists by my sides.
"I'm sure we can find another story-"

"You don't fucking get it!" I snapped, flexing my fingers in fear I would punch him in the face, "It's not as simple as finding another story when Craig only gave us today!"
Anger began to bubble within, causing my muscles to quiver while my heart pounded violently against my chest. *His job may also be on the line, but he will **always** have his parents to fall back on!*

Unable to rein in my acrimony a moment longer, I erupted like a volcano, "I can't pay the fucking rent due next week, never mind the bills, food shopping, and fuel! We're having to get food stamps just to make sure the kids are fed, and Harper's eating whatever they don't while I'm surviving on coffee and biscuits in the fucking office!"

A wave of emotions flitted across JJ's face, but I was far from done and continued my tirade, "On top of that, we've got another baby on the way, so fuck knows how we're gonna manage when we can barely survive as it is! So I can't afford not to have a job, unlike **you**!" My last comment visibly struck a nerve, but JJ remained quiet as he pressed a fist against his lips.
I shouldn't have said that...

"Look, JJ, I didn't mean-" I began, but he cut me off with a raise of his hand.

"I know what you meant." He said in a strangled tone, "You're not the first person, and you won't be the last." He then shook off his hurt and forced a smile, "Let's find a way inside then."
I was completely taken aback by his response. *Does... Does he mean it?...*

Clearing my throat, I wondered, "Are you sure?"

"Positive." He swiftly replied, "But promise me one thing,

yeah?"

"What?..." My voice trailed off as I scrubbed a hand through my hair.

"You tell me everything next time, alright?" He pressed, placing a consoling hand on my shoulder, "We're the bestest of buds, and it pisses me off that you feel you can't even talk to me."

"People have got their own shit going on; they don't need mine on top of it." I pointed out, quickly shutting down the conversation by shaking off his hold.

Turning my attention back upon the building, I said, "Let's split up and find a way inside."

"Alright, Fred." JJ grinned, "Want me and Scoob to go this way-" He gestured to the right with a nod, "While you, Daphne, and Velma go that way?" He then pointed to the left.

I merely stared at him, unimpressed. *Why does everything have to be a joke with him?*

When he didn't get the reaction he wanted, JJ threw his arms up in exasperation, grumbling, "Jeeez, lighten up!"

He then pulled a packet of cigarettes out of his tracksuit bottoms, mumbling through the one he stuffed in his mouth, "Call me if you find a way in, okay?"

I nodded before advancing on the gothic terrace to the left of the entrance block.

I began checking the bars on the lower windows, hoping they might be loose or rotten, but I had no luck when I reached the grand building at the end. *Fuck it...* I fumed, scrubbing a hand through my hair whilst traipsing around to the other side. *Perhaps there's a back door or somethi- Wait, how far back does this go?!* I gaped, staggering to a halt when I realised another gothic terrace was joined to the building, expanding further back where another grand structure was attached. *Is it like a massive square or something?*

Taking a step forward, a thud was heard underfoot. Gazing down, I saw what looked like splintered remains of a wooden board hidden amongst the tall blades of grass. *What the?* Then it dawned on me. *Is it what I think it is?* Peering up, I couldn't contain my excitement when I spotted an unboarded window along the top of the terrace; the bars misshapen. *Thank God I found a way in!* But my issue now was- *How the hell am I gonna get up there?* Unless there was a ladder or some boxes hidden in the grass, I had no means of getting to the window.

There must be something! How else did other people get inside? I glanced around for something – anything – to give me an idea, but there was no sign that anyone had ever attempted to climb up. *Then how the hell did they get in?* Flitting my attention to the grand building at the far end, I wondered whether that one had an access door. *There must be other doors in this place, not just the entrance.* That deliberation gave me the motivation I needed to go and have a look.

I jogged all the way down, but it didn't help I was a smoker and avoided exercise like the plague; I was out of breath before even making it halfway. *I really need to stop smoking...* When I finally reached the building, I had to rest against the boarded-up bay window for longer than I would like to admit, my breaths rasping painfully in my chest. I used this opportunity to quickly peer around but couldn't see a door. *Hopefully, there's one 'round the back.* If not, I had no idea what I was going to do.

Once I caught my breath, I made my way round the side towards the back, relieved to see what appeared to be a fire door. *I just need to move this out the way.* I pondered, eyeing up the commercial wheelie bin that was blocking it. Mustering up all my strength as it felt pretty weighty, I forcefully pushed it away. *What the fuck's in it?! And why's it blocking the fire exit?* Curiously opening the lid, I took a peek inside and saw a metal trolley, two crushed wheelchairs, and about a dozen books. Closing the lid with an audible thud, I turned for the door and grasped the silver knob, twisting it several times, but it was locked. *Oh for fuck's sake... What am I gonna do now?!* Then I eyed the wheelie bin once more. *I guess I've found a way to get to the window...*

I had no idea how long it had taken me to push the bin to the unboarded window, but my lungs were burning, and I could have sworn I pulled both calf muscles. *I **really** need to stop smoking!* I gasped, folding my arms on top of the bin and resting my head, taking a few moments to catch my breath. When it no longer felt like little needles were jabbing into my chest, I stepped back to judge the distance from the top of the bin up to the window. *I think I can make it... It looks about six-*

odd feet, maybe a bit more... I was an inch shy of six foot, so I knew I could reach the ledge even if I had to jump.

Clambering up on the bin, I stretched for the window ledge but could only just touch it with my fingertips.

I then readied myself to jump when someone shouted, "**WHAT ARE YOU DOING?!**"

A scream escaped me when they tried to violently shake the wheelie bin, but it was too hefty.

"Jesus fucking Christ!" I panicked, glaring down at JJ, who had burst into a fit of hysterical laughter.

"I **knew** I could scare you!" He rejoiced, bouncing from foot to foot with pure excitement; I couldn't help but shake my head as a tut left my lips.

When he had calmed down, JJ commented, "I see you found a way in." His attention turned skyward towards the unboarded window.

Shrugging, I replied, "Maybe. I guess it depends if it's unlocked. Otherwise, we'll have to try and break it."

"Well, there's only one way to find out." He grinned, gesturing with a nod towards the window, "Off you go then, Spiderman."

Shifting my focus back upon the ledge, I jumped up and grabbed it easily, now holding onto one of the bent bars with my right hand. I then brought my knees up to rest on the ledge whilst trying to open the window with my left hand. It felt a little stiff, but I knew it would open with some force.

"Is it unlocked?" JJ called up, and I replied without glancing down, "Yeah, it's just stu-"

WHOOSH! The window suddenly flew open as a gasp escaped me; I almost tumbled inside but managed to keep my balance.

"You alright, bud?!" JJ hollered whilst I still held onto the bar with trembling hands, feeling slightly shaken.

"Yuh-Yeah, I'm fine." I called down, but even I could hear the tremor in my voice.

Shaking off my fright, I peered inside the darkened room; the only light source was from the open window. From what I could tell, the entire wall to my right was once a massive bookshelf but now stood bare. Part of the ceiling lay in ruins on the carpeted floor, hiding most of the books scattered like shrapnel.

"What do you see?" JJ queried as I carefully clambered inside, trying to avoid the debris from the wall to my left.

Photo frames were smashed beneath the rubble, along with what I presumed was a dark wood desk.

"Erm..." I murmured more to myself, squinting to better see through the dimness, spotting a splintered and cracked door directly across from me.

Was this an office? A meeting room? I deliberated, glancing over at a wrecked, leather-looking sofa near the bookshelf as I walked across the room.

"Read me..." A voice unexpectedly whispered that sounded neither male nor female.

I could practically feel it vibrate throughout my body, instilling me with an indescribable fear. *Garghhh, that's creepy!* I shuddered before realising who the culprit was.

Glaring over my shoulder, I growled in annoyance, "What the fuck you playing at..." But I trailed off when I realised JJ was nowhere to be seen, doubt replacing my irritation.

Was I just hearing things?

"Read me..." The voice whispered again; it came from the debris by the massive bookshelf, somehow echoing around the room like a discordant harp.

Wait, is someone trapped in here?! I worried, about to holler for JJ to call for help; however, my concerns abruptly dissipated as I was drawn to the voice like a moth to a flame.

Where is it? I dropped to my knees with an audible thud once I was by the bookshelf. *Where is it?!* I was numb to the debris cutting into my palms while desperately rummaging for the voice. *I need it!* Then I felt something warm and wet trickle down my hands, but I didn't care. ***Want** it!* Then I finally found it, a worn leather-bound book. ***MINE!***

"Read me." The voice beckoned once more, resounding through the office devoid of emotion.

But, before I could finally touch its soft, enticing leather, a masculine voice wondered, "What are you looking at?"

My head snapped over to the window where JJ now stood. *No, it's mine!* I possessively growled, hiding it with a slab of rubble.

"Nothing." I hurriedly said as I rose to my feet, not giving him a chance to speak before gesturing to the door with a nod, "Let's take a look around."

I didn't wait for him to reply before trying the door, hissing in pain when the cold, metal handle touched my palm. *Why does my hand hurt? And why's it sticky?*

"You alright, bud?" JJ pried when he came to stand beside me, both of us gazing down at my bleeding hands.

How did I do this? I couldn't remember, so I quickly wiped them down my trouser legs.

"Yeah, I'm fine." I nodded, trying the door again, which opened with a spine-tingling groan.

God, it's so dark! I griped, unable to make anything out even when I took a couple of apprehensive steps; the light from the room now behind me didn't help either. *Where's my torch?* I wondered, patting down my pockets before remembering I had left my bag in the car. *Great...* I uttered, blindly taking a further step so JJ could make his way out of the room.

"Whoa, it's dark out here!" He gasped, "Haven't you got your torch?"

"Left it in the car." I replied with a shake of my head.

"What would you do without me?" He humorously queried, switching his on and lighting up a dilapidated, narrow corridor.

No wonder we couldn't see... I mulled, clocking the boarded-up windows along the wall across from us.

"So, what now?" JJ enquired while shining the torch from left to right, illuminating the smashed glass scattered across the rotten, cracked floorboards.

"Well, that Doctor Sasin guy put this place into lockdown." I began, "So if we can find his office, we may find out why he did it."

No one has ever found out why. I mulled, feeling a wide grin spread across my face. *Our story will be massive if we figure it out!*

"You make it sound so easy..." JJ murmured, causing my smile to falter when he carried on, "This place is fucking massive!" He gestured around with the torch before pointing it at the room behind us, "With any luck, this is his office."

Yeah, but what are the chances?...

Glancing at the nameplate on the door, I shook my head, "This one belonged to a Doctor Erik Kröger."

Huh, same name as that German doctor who specialises in bionic prosthetics.

"Now what do we do?" JJ questioned, "We can't exactly split up." He held up the torch, indicating we only had the one.

"Well, it **must** be up here somewhere." I adamantly replied, "I guess we've just got to check all the rooms."

"Again, you make it sound so easy..." He muttered, his negativity starting to grind my gears.

Inhaling a few steady breaths, I peered left where a splintered desk had been propped diagonally across the hallway. *Well, I guess we're not going that way...* We wouldn't even be able to climb over or under as upturned wheelchairs and bent gurneys were in the way, creating a barricade. *Someone really didn't want anyone to get through...*

Shifting my attention to the right, I noticed a busted door at the end of the hallway. I presumed it was part of the grand building I had passed before finding the unboarded window.

"Let's check all the offices down this way." I suggested, spotting what appeared to be another hallway to the left of the broken door when JJ shone the torch.

"The sooner we find it, the better." He commented with a shaky voice, clearly uncomfortable being in this building.

The floorboards groaned underfoot as we advanced on the door; I couldn't help but wonder what had happened as it appeared to have been bulldozed into. The torchlight then glinted against the nameplate where DR. ELON HAILEY was engraved in a bold font. *Fuck it!* I cursed, peering down the darkened corridor to the left to see where that led.

"Who's he?" JJ piped up; I followed his line of sight back upon the nameplate.

"Haven't a clue." I shrugged.

I then made my way down the corridor when JJ shone the torch, noting it was much wider and the windows on either side were boarded up. *It doesn't look like there's any offices down here...* I pondered, a crunch underfoot stilling me in my tracks.

"You know it'll be like trying to find a needle in a haystack." JJ clarified as I lifted my foot, the torchlight reflecting off the smashed photo frame I had accidentally stepped on.

I should've just told him to wait in the car... I uttered, clenching my jaw to stop myself from snapping.

Ignoring him, I pressed onwards to the end of the hallway, spotting a door to my right that I guessed was part of the grand building, similar to Doctor Hailey's office. Another corridor to my left was barricaded with wheelchairs, gurneys, and what appeared to be a splintered bookcase. When JJ finally shone the torch on the door, I couldn't help but smirk when I saw the nameplate.

"Well, here's your needle." I mocked, gesturing to the name engraved in a bold font: DR. FREDERICK SASIN.

"Why do you think he locked everyone in?" JJ pondered as we entered the lair of the traitorous doctor.

Shrugging, I gazed around the ravaged office, trying to decide where to search first.

"Hopefully we'll find out." I replied while clambering over a fallen filing cabinet; the desk lying sideways in the middle of the room had caught my eye.

"And if we don't?"

I immediately took a deep breath, holding it in. *He's really starting to piss me off...* I grumbled, staring over my shoulder at him, the torch practically blinding me.

Once JJ lowered it, I exhaled the breath in one big puff before suggesting through gritted teeth, "Then I guess we'll search some of the other offices."

"And if we find nothing then?" JJ pried further.

His negativity ignited the anger within, and I couldn't stop myself from snapping in a deep baritone, "Then we'll just go home like you fucking want, okay?!"

I didn't give him a chance to answer before shifting my attention back to the desk, crouching down to search the drawers. *My fucking God!* I fumed, vaguely aware of him sheepishly sifting through one of the upright filing cabinets. *And everyone says I'm a pessimist!*

The first two drawers hadn't proved fruitful; however, I found a document in the last drawer titled '**Solution To The Mentally Insane**'. *What's this?* Quickly skimming it, I realised it was a thesis written by Doctor Sasin. *How the fuck did he get away with this?!* I gaped, horrified to read he had illegally treated his patients.

"Hey, there's a patient in here with the same name as you!" JJ piped up, distracting me, "It had fallen behind the drawer with a few others."

Rising to my feet, I pocketed the document while curiously asking, "Really? There's not many Travis's I can think of."

"No, the same surname as you." He corrected, and that was an even greater surprise as I had never met anyone with the

surname '**Moon**' who wasn't related.
I wonder if Nan knew them?

"Bring that file with you." I said, wanting to flick through it later, "Other than that, have you found anything else?" I then peered around, realising all storage units had been emptied.

"Just those patient files." JJ replied, tucking the record underneath his arm, "Nothing to suggest why he locked everyone in."

"Damn it..." I uttered under my breath, weaving my hands into my hair and giving it a sharp tug.
We've only got two other offices to check before we either give up or have to figure out a way to get through all that stuff blocking the corridors.

Lowering my hands, I suggested, "Let's check out that Doctor Hailey's office."

"Sure, but did you want me to grab those other files real quick?"
I thought about it briefly before nodding, "Can't hurt to grab them, I guess."
JJ then buried his hand down the back of the cabinet, so I wandered into the hallway, my eyes somewhat used to the dark.

Why am I even bothering with this?... I murmured, my ribs tightening as doubt crept in. *No one else has figured out this story, so why did I think I could?...* I began mindlessly walking toward Doctor Hailey's office, my feet shuffling against the floorboards. *We could've spent this time finding a worthwhile story, but I just had to be stupid because I think I know best...*

"Hey, bud! Wait up!" JJ hollered before the thud of footsteps rapidly gained on me.
Turning to better face him once I reached Doctor Hailey's office, I heard the floorboards groan in protest. *What the?...* Then it happened all too quickly. I watched with wide, horrified eyes as the floor split open like a massive, gaping mouth.

"JOSH!" I bawled when he disappeared through the broken floorboards, his own cry echoing around the derelict asylum.
Oh my God! What if he's hurt?! Or dead?!
Charging over to the hole in a blind panic, I screamed once I reached the edge, "JOSH?!"
Then I saw the torch roll just out of sight, causing my heart to thud in my chest like a jackhammer. *Please don't be dead!*

"JOSH?!" I wailed once more before hearing someone wheeze, as if they were struggling to catch their breath.
"Josh?!" I desperately called before seeing something move in the darkness, reaching for the torch, and I released a huge breath when I saw he was alive.
Thank God he's okay! But my relief swiftly vanished when I noticed blood ooze through his left trouser leg like ink seeping into a piece of parchment. *Shit, has he broken his leg?!* I had no idea how to get down to him, never mind what to do with a broken leg. *I need to call an ambulance!*

"Just stay there!" I urged, pulling my mobile out of my jeans pocket, "I'm gonna call for help!"
My heart sank when I saw I had no signal. *Shit!* Biting my bottom lip, I didn't know what to do. *I can't leave him!* But I knew I had to as I had no way of getting down to him.
"Just wait there; I'll be back in a minute!" I promised.
"Trust me, I ain't going nowhere!" JJ hollered with a humourless laugh.
"I'll be right back!" I vowed again, charging down the corridor towards the office with the unboarded window.

I just need to call the police, tell them everything, and I'm sure they'll send an ambulance and the fire brigade! I reassured, my throat feeling constricted as the worry for my friend practically consumed me.

Glass and debris skidded across the floorboards when I came to a sliding halt just before Doctor Kröger's office. Grabbing the doorframe to steady myself, I flew inside only to stagger to a halt, my shoes scuffing against the light brown carpet. *What the fuck?!* I couldn't believe my eyes as I stared around the now intact room.

The massive bookshelf to my left was filled to the brim with books. A fresh-looking leather sofa was next to it, facing into the room, its back pressed against the wall to my left beside the door. I couldn't stop myself from touching it, refusing to believe all of this was real until my fingertips stroked the soft leather, causing a lump to form in my throat. *What the actual fuck is going on?!* I gaped, now peering at the two matching leather chairs opposite in the far left-hand corner; a round, dark wood coffee table was between them. *This... This* ***can't*** *be real!* I declared, vigorously shaking my head.

I then spotted the once-smashed photo frames hanging along the cream wall to my right. Half a dozen filing cabinets were underneath, partially hiding the dark wood panelling fitted to the lower half of the wall. *I... How... What the...* I faltered, unable to comprehend the scene before me as there was no way this could be real.

Movement then caught my eye. I soon noticed a dark-haired man sitting across from me behind his desk, which was just in front of the window I had climbed through not too long ago. *I... I **must** be dreaming!*

Chapter Two

I'm not a patient!

"Vat are you doing here?" The man questioned in a thick, German accent, peering up from his paperwork.
I merely stared at him, baffled. *It's a dream! It's just a dream!* But it felt too real to be a dream. *Did I fall through the floor and hit my head?* I began to wonder; it was the most plausible explanation I could think of. *Yes, that must be it! I've just hit my head!*

"I zaid '**Vat are you doing here?**'." The man repeated while rising to his feet, gaining my attention as he buried his hands inside his black slacks.
His white doctor coat was startling against the sunlight pooling in through the window behind him; an equally white shirt fitted with a black tie was tucked into his trousers.

"Er... Errrrr..." I croaked, apprehensively gripping my hands together.

"You schouldn't be here." He angrily commented, a wave of unease flitting across his youthful-looking face.

This... This isn't real! I reminded myself, closing my eyes and shaking my head, hoping the doctor would be gone when I opened them and everything would be back to normal. *It can't be real!* I persisted while slowly opening them, but everything was still in one piece; the doctor was now closer as he advanced on me.

I've got to get out of here! Spinning on my heels, I rushed back into the corridor, only to stumble in my tracks. *What the hell?!* I was now blinded by the sun's rays flooding in through the once boarded-up windows directly across from me. Blinking back the light, I could make out a courtyard down below. *No, no, no!* I panicked, now staring from my left to my right. The hallway was no longer ruined, its cream walls and dark wood panels matching the doctor's office. *This can't be real! It just can't!*

"Vat are you doing here?" I jumped when the German doctor spoke uncomfortably close.

I spun around where we now practically shared the same air, his blue eyes piercing me with curiosity as well as apprehension. "Schouldn't you be in zee recreation room?" He carried on, confusing me further.

Recreation room? I repeated with a furrowed brow. *Why would I-*

"There you are!" A woman's voice, deadlier than rattlesnake venom, sliced through my thoughts.

Staring down the hallway where I couldn't gain access earlier, I had to do a doubletake when my eyes landed on the serpent the voice belonged to. *Wow, she could be a model!* I gawked, blinking back my surprise before realising she was a nurse. *That's a very old-fashioned uniform...* I mulled, taking in her light blue dress, which reminded me of something the nurses would have worn during the war. It flowed off her slim build, accentuating her legs that went on for days.

As the nurse rapidly drew nearer, her brown heels clipping against the floorboards, I realised there was a darkness hidden behind her pretty face. *I say pretty lightly...* Now she was closer, I noted she had given herself a cost-effective facelift by pinning her golden blonde hair up into a ridiculously tight bun. Then I clocked her stone-cold, blue eyes. *Why's she staring at me like that?* The way she looked at me would put the collie stare to shame. Lastly, her smile reminded me of a reptile or some other kind of cold-blooded creature; it was something nightmares were made of.

"I've found him!" The nurse abruptly hollered over her shoulder just before two men built like brick shithouses emerged from a door on the left.

Fuuucking hell! I gaped, presuming they were orderlies judging by their all-white uniform. Their short-sleeved shirts were tucked into their slacks, emphasising their military cannon-like arms and nacho-shaped torsos.

"Where have you been?!" The nurse demanded as she glared up at me, snapping a hand onto her hip, "You know Doctor Sasin doesn't like to be kept waiting!"

It took a moment for her words to sink in, but when they did, I blurted, "What?"

Doctor Sasin? I repeated, furrowing my brow. *No, I must have heard her wrong.* Then I realised it didn't matter if I heard her wrong or not; this whole situation was just a figment of my unconscious imagination. *This is just a dream. None of this is real.*

"Vould you like help ezcorting him to Doctor Sazin?" The German doctor piped up as he slowly wrapped a hand around my bicep, squeezing it gently in anticipation.

What the hell is he doing?! I growled, about to push him off, but the nurse distracted me with a shake of her head.

"No, I don't need your help." She bluntly replied, gesturing to her two henchmen with a nod, "I'm pretty certain Tim and Tom are more than capable of escorting Mr Moon."

She blatantly stared me up and down, as if mentally comparing me to the orderlies who could easily give Stallone and Schwarzenegger a run for their money.

Reluctantly, the German doctor released me before the nurse snapped her fingers, a silent cue for the orderlies to snatch me up either side.

"What are you doing?!" I hawked, struggling against their impenetrable hold, "Let me go!"

They can't fucking do this! I proclaimed as the nurse marched off toward Doctor Sasin's office, the orderlies swiftly following with me in tow. I tried without much success to dig my heels into the slippery floorboards.

"You've made a mistake!" I asserted, "Let me go, and I won't file charges!"

They all ignored my outburst, so I heatedly demanded, "Why the fuck aren't you listening to me?! LET! ME! GO!"

I lashed out with my feet, trying to trip the orderlies, but the one on my left dug his fingernails into my arm, making me hiss in pain.

Wake up! I begged, desperate to get out of this nightmare. *Please, wake up!* But I didn't, and I was growing all the more terrified of how real this dream now felt. *I don't want to know what will happen in that office!* Determined not to find out, I peered up at the orderly who was still pinching my skin before down at his slightly tanned hand. It had clearly never seen the likes of soap, but I tried not to dwell on where it had been when I sunk my teeth into it. A howl of pain erupted from the orderly as he ripped his hand free, the tang of copper now lingering on my tongue.

Cupping his bleeding hand, the orderly raged, "YOU FUCKING CUNT!"

Then everything happened in the blink of an eye. He swung for me with his good hand; I managed to duck out of the way just in time before he punched his colleague in the chest, who released me when he staggered backwards into the wall with a thud. *Now's my chance!* With the orderlies and the nurse momentarily distracted, I charged back to the German doctor's office. He stood in the doorway, watching the ordeal unfold before him.

"**Move!**" I barked, but he didn't budge an inch, as if he were rooted to the spot in fear.

He's not gonna move! I realised, so I braced myself and shouldered past. He stumbled into the office with me but lost his balance, tumbling sideways and smacking his face against one of the filing cabinets. *Shit!* I panicked when he crumbled to the floor, presumably unconscious, but I assumed the worst. *I didn't mean it! I didn't mean to hurt him!* Then I heard the rush of footsteps in the corridor hone in on me. *I've got to go!*

Shooting the German doctor one last glance, I dashed to the window where my hope of escape was ripped from me. *What the fuck?!* Pressing the palms of my hands against the glass, I stared at the intact bars in dismay. *They... They weren't like that! They were bent! Broken! What the fuck is going on?!*

"Doctor Sasin's going to be so disappointed..." The venomous voice of the nurse murmured behind me.

Slowly, I turned around to see her standing in the doorway, evidently blocking the only escape route. The two orderlies were just the other side of the desk, the only thing stopping them from getting to me. *What do I do?!* I fretted, my eyes darting around the room for anything to defend myself with.

"I... I-I don't know who you think I am," I tremulously began, trying to reason with them, "But if you don't let me go, you'll be hearing from my lawyer!"

My threat just made the nurse burst into a brief moment of

maniacal laughter; the silence that instantly followed chilled me to my core.

A wicked smirk then hooked the corner of her lips as she said, "Tim, Tom, you know what to do."

The two orderlies advanced on me from either side of the desk, pincering me. *Fuck!* Shooting them a quick glance, I pressed my back against the window, trying to create as much distance between us as possible. But with nowhere to go, it rapidly diminished as they came to stand mere inches before me.

I should just apologise! I proclaimed, having to take several deep breaths in an effort to calm myself when the orderly on my right cracked his knuckles. *But I've done nothing wrong!* The thud of their boots against the floor matched my racing heart. *JUST FUCKING APOLOGISE!*

Anxiously staring between them, I cleared my throat and blurted, "I'm sor-"

BANG! The one who cracked his knuckles punched me clean across the face. My head unwillingly snapped to my left just in time to meet the unrelenting fist from the other. It felt like my soul had left my body as I crumbled to the floor, feeling physically sick from the throbbing pain in my face. *Don't be sick! Won't be sick!* I had to close my eyes when a headache pierced my brain, feeling like a thousand shards of glass slicing into it over and over.

"Pick him up." The venomous voice of the nurse commanded just before massive hands grabbed my arms, hoisting me to my feet where I didn't have the strength to stand.

The clip-clop of heels then pricked my ears when she drew near, abruptly stopping dead a few moments later. *What's she doing?* I wondered, not daring to open my eyes as the lights would only intensify my headache.

"Look at me." She instructed, but I didn't want to, "**LOOK AT ME!**"

The orderlies tightened their hold on my arms, causing such friction pain I wouldn't have been surprised if my skin was rubbed raw.

Begrudgingly, I opened them to see her leaning on the desk with the flats of her hands, leering at me with her reptilian smile that gave me the creeps.

"Next time, you do as you're told!" She growled before a wicked grin graced her lips, "Now, I feel we've kept Doctor Sasin waiting long enough."

She then clicked her fingers, an unspoken command for the orderlies to drag me back into the hallway. I didn't have the will or the strength to fight them again.

I just want to wake up! I desperately exclaimed as we headed down the long, wide corridor to Doctor Sasin's office. The nurse was at the head of our patrol after informing another about the German doctor. Just a few more steps, and we were outside Doctor Sasin's door; it felt like a lifetime since I was last here. **TAP! TAP! TAP!** The nurse gently knocked, and gentle wasn't a word I would have ever associated with her. I couldn't help but notice how her contemptible façade had drastically changed; she was almost- *Meek?* But then I disregarded that thought, putting it down to the merciless headache.

"Enter!" A hoarse voice hollered from the other side, sounding like someone who had been smoking their entire life.

The nurse then quietly opened the door and stepped inside, announcing, "Richard Moon is here to see you, Doctor Sasin."

Wait, what did she just call me? I wondered while the orderlies dragged my limp body into the office, a thick haze lingering in the atmosphere along with the stench of cigarette fumes. I peered at the nurse for confirmation as she quietly shut the door, her blue eyes locked onto a man sitting behind his desk, undoubtedly clad in the same garb as the other doctor.

At first glance, I thought the offices were identical, but I soon realised the furnishings were the other way around. The filing cabinets lined the left wall, while the massive bookshelf was on my right. The leather sofa was to the right of the window along the back wall, facing into the room. Two matching chairs with a coffee table were closer to the door but not quite in the bottom, righthand corner.

Then it dawned on me what the nurse had called this man: Doctor Sasin. *No, this must be some kind of joke!* I shifted my attention to the man in question. His dark brown hair was unfortunately inflicted with a vast receding hairline, making me guess he was in his early to mid-fifties. He hadn't looked up from his paperwork since we entered; his sculpted face unreadable as it was void of all emotion. I had never seen a photo of the doctor, so I wasn't sure if this was him.

Without looking up, Doctor Sasin ordered, "Sit him down."

He pointed the end of his pen to the chair directly across from him. It appeared to be made from wood with leather straps fitted on the arms and back, reminding me of a gas chamber chair. I inwardly groaned when the orderlies shoved me down, my headache intensifying against the abrupt movement. They then fastened the straps around my arms, leaving the back one unbuckled.

"Right, Richard..." Doctor Sasin began when the orderlies stepped out of sight, shifting his attention to me; I noticed his glacial blue eyes were just as dead as the rest of his face.

"Why are you late to our session?" He carried on, but I was more intrigued by the jagged-looking scar across his throat. *How did he get- Wait, session? What session?* I repeated, baffled. *What the hell is going on?!* Then I remembered this was just a dream. *It's **not** real.*

"Let me explain." The nurse unexpectedly piped up, now coming to stand on my left, "He decided to-"

"I'm talking to him, not **you**." Doctor Sasin intervened, not even bothering to glance at her; I knew then he was a force to be reckoned with.

I need to think carefully about what I'm gonna say if I don't want to piss him off.

"Look, there must be some kind of misunderstanding." I calmly explained, "I'm not a patient. I'm a journalist from News Brothers. My car's outside with my ID; I can **prove it**."

There was no reaction, nothing from Doctor Sasin. *Doesn't he believe me?*

"I've even got my driver's licence on me." I hastily added, "It's in my jeans pocket."

I gestured with a nod down at my trousers only to do a doubletake.

Wait, what the hell am I wearing?! I gawked at the baggy, dark blue trousers that appeared to be pocketless. *These aren't my clothes!* The accompanying snug, light blue shirt clung to my torso, the sleeves tight around my defined biceps. Then I spotted the dark-coloured shoes. *What the hell happened to my converses?! Why am I wearing grandad shoes?!*

"He's gotten worse..." Doctor Sasin muttered, gaining my attention and realising he was talking to himself.
His glacial blue eyes then focused on me once more as he leaned back in his leather-bound chair, scrubbing a hand across his clean-shaven jaw.
"The treatment obviously isn't working; we'll need to try something more..." His first sign of emotion was shown through a villainous, one-sided smirk, "Aggressive."
"Aggressive?!" I automatically echoed, shocked.
*What the hell does he mean by '**aggressive**'?!*
Shaking my head, I desperately insisted, "I'm **not** a patient! You've made a mistake!"
Ignoring my outburst, Doctor Sasin instructed the nurse, "Take him to the treatment room."
"**WHAT?!**" I hawked just before the orderlies practically ripped off the straps, hoisting me upwards and making me feel dizzy.
"What do you mean '**treatment room**'?!" I demanded but was ignored yet again.
Doctor Sasin focused solely on the nurse when he stated, "Deadman, you know what to do." That comment seemed to fill her with glee by the delight twinkling in her stone-cold eyes.
With a wicked grin of her own, she nodded, "As always, Doctor."

***

"PLEASE!" I screamed as the orderlies dragged me into a windowless room, my heart beating so hard it was giving me palpitations.
I had paid very little attention to where I had been taken; instead, I tried to fight my way free to no avail, resulting in a split lip and a bloody nose from the orderlies backhanding me.
"YOU'VE GOT TO BELIEVE ME!" I futilely carried on just as Nurse Deadman slammed the door behind us, snapping me back to my senses.
Only now did I become aware of the fully tiled white room I was standing in. *What the fuck is this room?!* Two rows of bathtubs faced one another lengthways with pipes fastened on either end. I quickly counted five tubs in each row. *Is... Is this a hydrotherapy room?...* I wondered, clocking the control

panels when Nurse Deadman advanced on the nearest along the right. She began turning a few of the dials, and the bathtub started to fill. *They're not gonna put me in, are they?* I worried, wriggling against the orderlies hold, but their ironlike grips intensified.

"Tim, Tom," Nurse Deadman spoke, that eerie smile gracing her lips as she ordered, "Strip him."

My heart suddenly plummeted, my head recoiling while staring at her with wide, disbelieving eyes. *'**Strip**'?!* I didn't get the chance to retaliate before the orderlies began yanking at my clothes, not caring they practically gave me friction burns when they ripped them off, discarding them on a pale blue unit next to the door.

"You're gonna regret this!" I vowed while the orderlies now firmly held me in place, the cold tiles underfoot chilling me to the bone.

My threat gained Nurse Deadman's attention. She merely stared at me in amusement before fiddling with the dials, the bath now filled to the brim. She then made her way back over; the clip of her heels against the floor echoed around the room before she came to stand in front of me.

What's she laughing at?! I seethed when she tittered to herself, blatantly staring my naked body up and down like I was a slab of meat hanging in a butcher shop window.

"What?!" I growled through gritted teeth, her evident wanton gaze not shifting even after an awkward amount of time.

"What the fuck you looking at?!" I snapped in a deep baritone, my body tensing in anger.

Reluctantly, Nurse Deadman's blue eyes circled up to meet mine, a coy grin pulling at her lips when she said, "Well, you're definitely not average, are you?"

What the hell?! I couldn't quite believe what she had said. Part of me wondered whether I had gone crazy as her lustful gaze abruptly vanished in the blink of an eye, replaced with apathy.

Diverting her attention up to the orderlies, Nurse Deadman instructed, "Put him in and fasten the sheets."

"NO!" I panicked when they dragged me towards the bathtub, my feet sliding on the tiles as I struggled against them, "LET ME GO!"

They soon got fed up with my will to fight and easily hoisted me off my feet, carrying me the rest of the way. There was a bit more of a kerfuffle when they tried putting me in the tub. I kept pushing myself backwards using my feet, but they swiftly grew wise, and one now held my legs while the other still grasped me by the arms.

"**FUCK!**" I gasped against the hot water when they finally managed to get me in; it wasn't excruciatingly hot, but I knew it would quickly get insufferable.

I tried again to clamber out, but one firmly held me down while the other threw a white sheet across the tub, using the straps and buckles fixed on either side to fasten it in place.

"You won't get away with this!" I assured, glowering at Nurse Deadman, who was hovering by the pale blue unit fiddling with a retro-looking stereo.

"When my lawyer hears about this, you're gonna be sucked dry of every fucking penny you have!"

A malevolent smirk hooked the corner of her lips as she glanced over at me, saying, "We'll be back shortly, Mr Moon." She then turned on the stereo; the strum of what sounded like a ukulele began to play obnoxiously loud. '**Tiptoooooe throoough the windooow, byyy the windoooow, that is where III'll be, come tiptoooe through the tulips with meeeeeeee!**'.

"NOOOOOOOO!!!" I furiously bellowed when Nurse Deadman and the orderlies left, my voice barely heard over the annoying music, "**YOU CAN'T FUCKING LEAVE ME LIKE THIS! I HAVE MY FUCKING RIGHTS!**"

***

I had no idea how long I had been left to endure the God-awful song on repeat, but I could feel my sanity slowly slip away. I tried to think of an escape plan, but it was hard to concentrate with the song perforating my eardrums and what was left of my soul. My heart was beating harder and faster; I felt I couldn't breathe in these sweltering conditions.

A despairing moan leaked from my lips just as the door opened, an appreciated distraction from the music. *Thank God she's back!* I gasped, feeling a little giddy that I would soon be out of the bath. Then I realised Doctor Sasin had entered, not Nurse Deadman and the two orderlies. Now he was no longer sitting behind his desk; I could tell Doctor Sasin was a tall man, which only added to the imposing presence he oozed.

"Deadman!" Doctor Sasin heatedly growled when he took a further step inside, visibly cringing when he shot the stereo an angered glance.
He clearly isn't a fan of the song either... I murmured before Nurse Deadman hurried inside, followed by the two orderlies.
"Turn that atrocious music off this instant!" He yelled, not waiting for her to reply before advancing on me.
A sigh of relief escaped me when the room fell into silence.

"Right, Richard." Doctor Sasin sternly began, crouching beside me on my left, "Now you've had time to mull over your actions; I have some questions for you."
Why does he keep calling me Richard?! I fumed, my temper readying to snap like a rubber band. *I've had enough of these people mistaking me for some guy called Richard!*
"Why were you late to our session? And why did you attack Doctor Kröger?" He carried on, the band within threatening to break at any given moment.
I didn't attack him, he got in my fucking way! I inwardly growled, my muscles quivering as anger rapidly consumed me.

"You've been a star patient up until now." Doctor Sasin commented, talking to me as if I were a child, "If something is the matter, why haven't you spoken to me and, instead, taken a drastic turn for the worse?" That last comment was what tipped me over the edge.

I was so fed up with no one listening to me, so the band within snapped, and I verbally exploded, "I told you, I'm **not** a patient, and my name **isn't** Richard!"
My outburst evidently took Doctor Sasin aback by the jerk of his head. I could tell I had triggered something by the callous gleam now in his glacial blue eyes, instilling me with an unspoken fear that I didn't understand.

After a long, drawn-out silence where I watched a throbbing vein pulse down his forehead, Doctor Sasin finally asked, "Then who are you if you aren't Richard?"

"Travis." I stated matter-of-factly, as if he should have known that all along, "My name is Travis Chase Moon."
I was shocked when he immediately laughed in disbelief, rising to his feet and towering over me.

"Just to clarify," Doctor Sasin started, gesturing with a raise of his hand for me to remain silent, "Your name isn't Richard, but you have the same surname?"

I shot him a bewildered look, blurting, "We do?"
Then I remembered when Nurse Deadman had referred to me as Mr Moon or Richard Moon. *What the hell is going on?!*

"This needs to be nipped in the bud as a matter of urgency." Doctor Sasin commented; I realised he was talking to himself as his glacial blue eyes looked off into the distance.
He then snapped himself out of his daze and turned to Nurse Deadman, saying, "You know what to do."

"Know what?!" I piped up, anxiously staring after him as he made a beeline for the door, "What does she know?!" But he just continued to ignore me.
I couldn't stand the churning sensation in my gut when my anxiety got the better of me. *I need to know!*
"WHAT DOES SHE KNOW?!" I desperately hollered again as he opened the door, "**WHAT DOES SHE KNOW?!**" But it slammed shut behind him, filling me with dread as now the only way I would find out was when it happened.

"Get him out." The venomous voice of Nurse Deadman distracted me; I peered over to see that spine-chilling, reptilian smile gracing her lips.

"What are you gonna do with me?!" I frantically asked.
My question may as well have fallen on deaf ears; she merely sauntered over to the bathtub directly on my right, turning the dials on the control panel to fill it up.
"What are you gonna do with me!" I demanded while the orderlies unfastened the sodden sheet covering me.
Why isn't she answering me?!

I could feel the elastic band within start to grow taut yet again.
"OIT!" I barked just as one of the orderlies tossed the sheet aside, the other grabbing me by the tops of my arms, "Why the fuck are you ignoring-"
THWACK! A drawn-out groan was the only thing I permitted to leave my lips when the orderly, who wasn't holding me, backhanded me across the face. The copper tang of blood now lingered on my lips.

While I was momentarily dazed, they hoisted me out of the steaming hot bath, and I was immediately struck with a severe light-headedness. *God, my head...* I inwardly moaned while black dots speckled my vision. My body then grew unbearably heavy, and I couldn't help but slump in the orderlies hold when a bout of nausea consumed me.

"The bath's now ready." Nurse Deadman piped up before the orderlies dragged me over, my vision barely back to normal when they hastily dunked me into its freezing depths. I couldn't stop the cry which escaped my hold; it was so excruciatingly painful that I thought my bones would shatter.

My hands shook so much that I couldn't stop them from fastening a new sheet in place, but that didn't stop me from begging, "Pluh-Please don't luh-leave me in here!"

I was ignored again, so I spoke a little louder, "Duh-Don't leave muh-me in here!"

That horrid smile grew on Nurse Deadman's lips as she sauntered past, gesturing with a nod for the orderlies to follow.

They can't leave me like this!

Struggling to still my chattering teeth, I desperately tried to reason with her one last time, "**PLEASE!**"

I watched with wide, hopeful eyes when she came to a standstill beside the door, peering over her shoulder at me.

"Pluh-Please don't luh-leave muh-me in here!"

Silence lingered in the atmosphere; I could practically hear the cogs turn in her head.

Unexpectedly, Nurse Deadman glanced up at the orderlies, saying, "I'll be out in a moment."

I would have been lying if I didn't admit I was stunned. *Is she really gonna let me out?*

Once they had left, I held my breath when she sauntered toward me, stupidly thinking she was heading to the control panel until she stopped beside the stereo.

"I almost forgot!" She wickedly grinned, fiddling with the dials until the strum of that ukulele played obnoxiously loud yet again.

"We'll be back soon, Mr Moon." Nurse Deadman reassured, advancing to the door where my heart immediately sank.

"Don't go anywhere." She added over her shoulder before leaving; the slam of the door was like a slap to the face.

This... This can't be happening! I exclaimed just as that irritating voice began to sing. '**Tiptoooooe throough the windooow, byyy the windoooow, that is where III'll be, come tiptoooe through the tulips with meeeeeeee!**'.

***

'OOOHHHHHHHHHHHHHHHHHHHHHHHHHHHHHHHHHHHH!!!'.
The song hit that annoying peak for the forty-something time. *At least I think it's forty...* I couldn't be sure as I had lost count roughly around the twenty mark; it was the only thing distracting me from the intolerable coldness that made me feel like I was slowly dying. *Or maybe it's forty-five?...*

The door then opened with a squeak, and in stepped Doctor Sasin, who was closely followed by Nurse Deadman and the orderlies. Now I was no longer distracted; I was immediately fixated on the excruciating coldness that consumed every inch of me. *I can't take it anymore!*

"GUH-GET ME OUT!" I begged through chattering teeth, and Doctor Sasin swiftly replied while advancing on me, "Not until I've asked you some questions."

The room then fell into silence; I was vaguely aware Nurse Deadman had turned the stereo off while the orderlies hovered by the door.

"PLUH-PLEASE!" I desperately beseeched, all sense of control now lost as the hope of warmth was just within reach, "Get muh-me out!"

My consistent pleading must have rubbed Doctor Sasin up the wrong way as he snapped, "You'll wait until **I** say you can get out!"

That throbbing vein had returned, zigzagging down his reddening face that oozed with animosity.

"Now," He began once he regained his impassive façade, towering over me, "Why were you late to our session?"

A tightness formed in my chest at that question, a frustrated snort escaping me as I heatedly retorted, "Buh-Because I'm not a **fuh-fucking** patient! Yuh-You've made a muh-mistake!"

"I'll ask you one last time." Doctor Sasin spoke in a deep, threatening undertone, "Why were you late to our session?"

"And I tuh-told you!" I bit back with bared teeth, "I'm nuh-not a puh-patient! I'm a journalist fruh-from Nuh-News Broth-"

"**No, you're not!**" He declared, pounding a fist against the bathtub and making me recoil; I honestly thought he was going to hit me.

Once he became detached from his emotions again, Doctor Sasin turned to Nurse Deadman, who was still lingering

beside the unit.
"Put him in solitary confinement!" He snapped, storming out of the hydrotherapy room without another word.

"You heard him!" Nurse Deadman commanded when the orderlies didn't move, "Get him out and take him to solitary confinement!"

Wait, what?! I panicked while the orderlies unfastened the sheet. *Solitary confinement?!* I repeated while one of them tossed the sodden sheet aside, the other grabbing me by the tops of my arms. *No, I need to get out of here!*

I readied myself to fight as soon as I was pulled out of the freezing water; however, going from such extremities was shockingly painful. *Oh my fucking God!* I inwardly gasped as my entire body throbbed in time to my beating heart. I immediately collapsed in the orderlies hold, unable to withstand my body weight. I couldn't even put one foot in front of the other when I was dragged over to the pale blue unit, which had open front cubbyholes; fresh towels, sheets, and uniforms were folded inside.

"Hurry up and get dressed!" Nurse Deadman ordered, thrusting a clean uniform in my chest when the orderlies released me, "I haven't got all day."

It was a struggle grasping the clothes, never mind putting them on. My hands were painfully hot, as if I were a child who had played in the snow without gloves, only to suffer the consequences when I returned to the warmth of my home.

"I'm trying!" I explained but wasn't quick enough as Nurse Deadman snapped, "Tim, Tom, get him dressed!"

The orderlies manhandled me into the clothes, treating me like a doll that had been abused by far too many children at nursery.

When they had finally managed to make me look somewhat presentable, Nurse Deadman led the way and turned right out of the hydrotherapy room. I used this opportunity to create a mental map of the asylum. *Whereabouts are we?* I mulled, glancing out the barred windows to my left, which overlooked the asylum grounds I didn't recognise.

We then reached the end, and the only way to go was right. Lights flickered overhead as we marched down the new, windowless hallway with cream walls and a dark, hardwood floor. Then I realised this place looked nearly identical with its labyrinthine corridors and bland colour scheme. *How the fuck am I gonna get out of here when it all looks the fucking same?!* I had planned to rely on my photographic memory, but now I merely stared on in despair as we passed another indistinguishable hallway on either side.

A gated door soon loomed ahead. I instantly knew we had reached solitary confinement when I saw a male guard stationed on the other side, not that the plaque above with '**SOLITARY CONFINEMENT**' in big, bold font was a dead giveaway. I couldn't see much through the gate except a heavy-looking metal door directly opposite. It wasn't until we were granted access that I realised we had entered via a side passage, now noticing more metal doors lined the corridor on either side. The main gated entrance was at the end of the hallway to my right, while to my left led to a dead-end.

"Name?" The guard queried, retrieving a clipboard from a small, wooden table while Nurse Deadman replied bluntly, "Richard Moon." Which immediately irked me.

"I told you," I growled through gritted teeth, "My name **isn't**-" **THWACK!** One of the orderlies backhanded me across the face, splitting my lip again. An internal moan rumbled to the surface, but I refused to release it.

"Number fifteen is available." The guard commented, not once peering up from his clipboard while gesturing left with a nod.

That was when I noticed two names on his list had a warning next to them in red: a Zedekiah and a Curtis. *Why can't they be let out?*

"Leave it blank." Nurse Deadman instructed before the guard could write my name down.

He didn't argue and merely discarded the clipboard back on the table.

The orderlies then hauled me towards the impending metal door, my gaze darting around in an attempt to absorb everything for my mental map, but I just couldn't focus.

"NO!" I shrieked, not having the fight in me anymore to fend them off.

This is just a dream! I insisted, my shoes squealing against the floorboards as I dug my heels in. *I'll wake up soon, and all of this would've been just a dream!* Albeit a horrible, painful one, but I didn't care as long as I woke up. *Now would be a pretty good time!*

Once we reached number fifteen, Nurse Deadman opened the door. I noticed the fully tiled white room was smaller than Harry Potter's cupboard under the stairs. *How do they expect me to fit in-* A shocked gasp escaped me when the orderlies shoved me inside. I narrowly missed the hard-looking bed made of off-white slabs to my right, catching myself on the metal toilet in the far left-hand corner a foot away from the bed.

"See you in the morning." The venomous voice of Nurse Deadman echoed behind me.

Spinning round, I saw that horrid smile grace her lips as she grasped the door.

"Wait!" I pleaded, but she swung it shut before I could make a dash for freedom, and I was immediately plunged into darkness. The sound of a key turning in the lock made my heart plummet, and I couldn't stop the terrified scream that escaped me,
"**DON'T LEAVE ME IN HERE!**"

Chapter Three

Just keep doing what you're doing

Have they forgotten about me?! I fretted, repeatedly rubbing my face while sitting on the hard, stone-cold bed. I had no idea how long I had been left; it felt like days, weeks even. It didn't help that I had nothing to pass the time, so my mind wandered. *What am I gonna do if they've left me?! I've no way of getting outta here!* Pitch-black infested every inch of the cell; I couldn't even see my hands if I brought them up in front of me.

A sudden, overwhelming sense of dread then smothered me when Harper and the kids came to mind. *Will they think I've abandoned them?! No longer love them?!* I panicked, going to fiddle with my wedding band, but it was no longer there, not even a mark to show it ever existed. *What the?* I couldn't even begin to understand what was going on. Grasping the sides of my head, I tried to regain control when everything felt as if it were spiralling out of my hands. *This can't be happening! This **can't** be happening!* I insisted, squeezing my eyes tightly shut so the darkness could no longer taunt me.

*I **will** get out of here!* Jumping to my feet, I rushed in the direction where I vaguely remembered the metal door was, ruthlessly pounding a fist against it.

"LET ME OUT!" I hollered, banging on it again and again and again, not caring my throbbing knuckles felt wet and sticky.

"**GET ME THE FUCK OUTTA HERE!**" I screamed at the top of my lungs, now smashing both fists desperately against the door.

Then I faintly heard the clip-clop of heels before the peephole opened with a clatter, momentarily blinding me when

light pooled in. I didn't get a chance to make out who they were before it was shuttered once more.
"**WAIT!**" I wailed in despair, "DON'T LEAVE ME IN HERE!"
A key turned in the lock before the door opened, light from the hallway blinding me again. Squinting against the harsh brightness, I could barely make out the silhouette of whoever had opened my cell.

"Get him out." A venomous voice instructed, and I instantly knew it belonged to Nurse Deadman.
Her two henchmen then reached inside before my eyes had adjusted, yanking me out where she shut the door behind me. As I was dragged down the hallway towards the main gated entrance, I asked, "Where are we going?"

"The recreation room." Nurse Deadman bluntly replied, "Doctor Sasin will see you tomorrow to discuss what happened yesterday."
Not if I can get out of here before then... I murmured as the orderlies pulled me to a standstill, leaving Nurse Deadman to talk with the guard.

When we were finally allowed out, Nurse Deadman led the way, turning left into a wide corridor where the dark, hardwood floor and cream walls continued. I couldn't help but notice it shared a similar resemblance to solitary confinement with the metal doors on either side. There was also a gated entrance up ahead. *How the hell am I gonna get out of here?* I pondered, noting the sheer number of staff we passed. Then I spotted no guard stationed at this gate; Nurse Deadman had a key that she unlocked it with. Through the bars, I could see a dead-end a few feet beyond; the only way to go was left where daylight appeared to pool in from somewhere.

Once she had unlocked the gate, Nurse Deadman gestured for the orderlies to bring me through with a sharp wave of her hand.
"Take him straight to the recreation room." She instructed, "I won't be far behind."
She then proceeded to lock the gate while the orderlies herded me down the new corridor. Sunlight flooded in through the barred windows on either side, and I soon got a distinct feeling I recognised where I was.

Isn't that the courtyard I saw upstairs? I mulled, staring at it through the window to my left. I then peered out the window to my right, spotting a gravel track. *That's the front! That's the fucking entrance to this place!* Glancing further down the corridor, I saw a grand archway that I presumed led to the entrance block.

Now's my chance to escape! I didn't consider the number of staff milling up and down, never mind what I would do once I reached the massive gate outside; I just went into fight or flight mode. Without thinking, I abruptly dropped to my knees, causing the orderlies to lose their balance as well as their hold on me. While they were momentarily distracted, I scrambled to my feet and dashed for the archway, the taste of freedom now within reach. *They're gonna regret everything they did to me!*

"**STOP HIM!**" The shrill voice of Nurse Deadman echoed behind me, gaining the attention of staff wandering the corridor.

The staff didn't get the chance to react before I skidded under the archway, my shoes screeching against the floorboards just before- **BANG!** I was sent flying backwards when I collided with something, knocking the wind out of me when I hit the floor with an oof. Whatever I had bumped into hit the reception desk with a mighty thud; it was in the middle of the room, acting as a barrier between the public and the asylum.

Urgh... A groan leaked from my lips as I leaned on my elbows, staring around the appointed reception area in a daze. It was well-lit, with barred windows on either side, then I noted the door to freedom directly opposite the desk. *What happened?...* I wondered just before a scream erupted from the receptionist. I followed her wide, bulbous eyes to the figure lying motionless beside her desk. *Shit!* I gasped, recognising him as the German doctor. My chest became so unbearably tight; it felt like I couldn't breathe when I saw blood trickle down his face.

"I-I-I didn't mean it!" I insisted to the receptionist, staggering to my feet, "I swear, I didn't mean it!"

I hastily backed out into the corridor. *What the fuck am I gonna-* **THWACK!** An unrelenting force smacked me around the face, sending me spiralling to the floor in a dazed heap. *What the?...* I was then snatched up by the front of my shirt and hoisted into the air, my feet dangling a few inches as I came face to face with one of the orderlies.

"I-I didn't mean it!" I declared, but I wasn't sure if he had even noticed the unconscious – *Please don't be dead!* – doctor now behind him.
The other orderly then appeared beside him. I was honestly fearful for my life by the way they just stared at me like vultures deciding where to peck first. *Oh God, they're gonna kill me! What the hell am I gonna do?!*

Surprisingly, my prayers were answered by an articulate man's voice coming from behind me, "Put him down this instant!"
When the orderly made no move to release me, the articulate man snapped, "**Now!**"

"Ah-ah-aaaah!" The venomous voice of Nurse Deadman stopped the orderly just as I felt his hold lessen.
She then appeared not even a second later, coming to stand alongside her henchmen while looking at whoever the guy was behind me.

"I don't think so, Doctor." She firmly stated, "After all, he's not your patient."

"And neither is he yours." The articulate doctor responded, his tone dropping an octave as he added, "You fail to remember that this is my hospital, not yours. **You** are **my** employee, so you shall do as I say."

"And you fail to remember it's not just **your** hospital!" She heatedly retorted.

I had expected an argument to pursue, but Nurse Deadman merely shifted her stone-cold, blue eyes over to the orderly holding me.
"You heard him." She said, "Let the patient go."
He released his hold without checking I was standing on my own two feet, making me crumble to the floor with a thud. I didn't get the chance to stand before someone dressed in doctor garb grabbed me by the arm, yanking me up where I stood a couple of inches taller than him.

"Cora," He began to Nurse Deadman; I realised he was the articulate doctor, and I could finally put a voice to a face, "I need you, Tim and Tom to take Erik to the infirmary."
I knew he was referring to the German doctor, who was still lying motionless on the floor, as his scarily dark brown eyes were locked on him the entire time. That was when I clocked the jagged scar on his face. *Whoa!* It zigzagged down his right eye

from his brow to just above his lip. *How did he get that?!* But then I wasn't sure if I wanted to know.

There was a presence about him that screamed evil. I put it down to his chilling, hatchet face adorned with a dark and grey specked goatee, matching his coiffed, receding hair that would put Dracula's to shame.

"Bethany," He carried on, his dark, penetrating gaze shifting to the receptionist knelt beside the German doctor, "Put a closed sign up. We can't risk tarnishing our name if members of the public were to bear witness."

By now, I was aware other staff members had gathered, watching on with mixed emotions.

The articulate doctor had also noticed everyone staring, and he snapped, "What are you all doing standing around?! Get back to work!" And they hastily dispersed like a ripple on the water.

"As for you," He growled up at me, "You're coming with me!"

He sharply yanked me back in the direction I had come from, only for Nurse Deadman to pipe up, "Excuse me, Doctor!" She seethed, not carrying on until we turned back to her, "But he is not your patient, so I must insist he is taken to Doctor Sasin for his punishment!"

Punishment?! I panicked, my hands anxiously clenching and unclenching by my sides.

"**I** don't care what **you** insist." The articulate doctor retorted in a sharp tone, "My hospital. My rules. Now, I must **insist** that you do as you're told and take Erik to the infirmary." He gestured with a nod towards the unconscious German doctor before dragging me back through the gated hallway, passing solitary confinement. *Where the hell is he taking me?!* I fretted, clearing my throat as it was beginning to feel constricted. *And what is he gonna do to me?!*

Feeling uneasy, I anxiously insisted, "I didn't mean it! I swear, I didn't mean to hurt him!"

He still hadn't said anything when we reached another unguarded, gated door at the other end. *I should make a break for it.* I pondered, feeling confident that he was no match compared to the two orderlies. *But what if I get caught again? What will happen then?* Just the thought of another hydrotherapy session sent shivers up my spine. *No, I can't risk getting caught again.*

While the doctor locked the gated door behind us, I quickly gazed around. I had no idea where the entry in the left-hand corner led, but I did recognise the corridor to my right. The massive barred window along the left wall overlooking the asylum grounds was what greeted me when I stepped out of the hydrotherapy room yesterday.

He then pocketed his keys with a clink before dragging me through the door in the left-hand corner; it led to a stairwell and- *Is that a fire door?!* Then I remembered the one I had found round the back of the asylum. *Is it the same one?* A new spark of hope ignited as I was pulled up the stairs to the first floor. *That's my way out of here!* But for now, I had to appease the doctor for fear of being tormented again.

Then something dawned on me when he opened the stairwell door, yanking me out into another corridor. *If that is the same fire door, then this must be the floor JJ and I broke into...* I peered down the hallway, spotting three doors along the right-hand wall while windows on the left overlooked the courtyard. There was a dead-end to my left, so the only way to go was right. The first door we passed had DR. GREGORY BUETER engraved on the nameplate, and the second had DR. TOBIAS SCANDURA. Then we came to the third door with DR. ERIK KRÖGER on the nameplate, confirming my suspicions. *It **is** the same floor!* I was now starting to get a mental layout of the asylum.

But then I remembered whose office was just right around the corner: Doctor Sasin's. *He's seriously not taking me there, is he?!* I couldn't bear the thought of seeing that man again. *What will he do to me when this guy tells him what happened?!*

"You've got to believe me!" I pleaded once more, "I didn't mean to hurt him!"

The doctor didn't say a word as he pulled me towards the end of the corridor.

"**PLEASE!**" I beseeched, digging my heels in, but he was surprisingly strong for a slightly built guy, "I swear, I didn't mean it!"

However, we didn't turn left down that wide hallway; instead, he opened the office door with DR. ELON HAILEY engraved on the plaque. I had a sense of déjà vu when I was wrenched into the office; I couldn't pinpoint how or why until I sat down in the gas chamber-looking chair, the doctor not bothering to strap me in. The room was identical to Doctor Sasin's; however, the filing cabinets lined the left wall while the massive bookshelf and furniture were to the right.

My attention then returned to the doctor when he wandered behind his desk. I presumed he was Doctor Hailey or didn't care about being in someone else's office. *Why is he ignoring me?* I deliberated, peering at the straps hanging down from my chair. *And why hasn't he restrained me?* But that question only led to more unanswered ones.

Glancing at Doctor Hailey when he sat down, I asked, "You believe me, don't you? You know I didn't mean to hurt-"

"Alright, that's enough!" He finally snapped, raising his hands in a stop gesture, "You're not winning any Oscars with me."

Oscars? I repeated, confused before realising. *He thinks it's all just an act! He doesn't believe me!* And my heart immediately sank.

"What happened yesterday?" Doctor Hailey queried, now leaning on his forearms as he stared at me with his dark, penetrating gaze, "We agreed you'd come and see me after your session with Fred."

Fred? Then I guessed he was referring to Doctor Sasin by his first name. *But why was I meant to go and see him afterwards?*

Furrowing my brow, I hesitantly explained, "I... I was put in solitary confinement..." And that was a sentence I never thought I'd have to say.

"Solitary confinement?" Doctor Hailey echoed, his face contorting into raw, ugly anger when I nodded.

Why does he care if I've been put in solitary confinement?

"And did Fred arrange for you to be put in there?" He pried in a deep baritone; the rolling tap of his impatient fingers against the desk filled me with an indescribable fear.

There was something about this doctor that immediately put me on edge.

When I didn't reply, Doctor Hailey's displeasure swiftly subsided, and he calmly empathised, "I can't even begin to imagine how difficult this must be for you, but I respect everything you're doing and putting yourself through."

Putting myself through? I repeated, my head flinching back slightly in shock. *What the hell is he on about?*

"But I need to know as it's against protocol." He explained, and I couldn't ignore the worry now blazing behind his dark gaze. *Why's it against protocol? What's the point of having solitary confinement if patients can't go in there?*

After a moment of silence, I confirmed, "Yeah, he told the nurse to take me there."

"Why?" Doctor Hailey inquired, but I couldn't bring myself to admit the truth, fearing he would also punish me.

They clearly all think I'm crazy for one reason or another... Saying I'm not who they think I am only adds fuel to the fire...

With a massive shrug, I muttered, "I dunno..."

My answer put Doctor Hailey on edge; he squinted hard at me before wondering, "What's wrong with you today? Why are you acting peculiar?"

Oh fuck, I said the wrong thing... But I didn't know how to respond. *I haven't a fucking clue how whoever I am usually acts!*

"I'm just, you know..." I murmured, saying the first thing that came to mind, "Tired... After the ordeal yesterday..."

Again, he stared intently at me, pursing his lips in thought. *Oh God, I've said the wrong thing again!*

I didn't think Doctor Hailey believed me until he replied, "Very well..." He shot me a sympathetic look before soothingly saying, "Hopefully, it won't be much longer, as we've almost got enough evidence. Just remember, you're helping a lot of people."

Wait, what?! I gaped, a sudden feeling of cold expanding within my core. *Evidence? Evidence for what? And how am I helping people?* I wanted to ask but knew I shouldn't. It was like a scratch I couldn't itch, persistent and unyielding.

"Anyway," Doctor Hailey sighed, rising to his feet where he winced in pain.

"Cor, my back..." He griped, shaking off his discomfort before carrying on, "As I was about to say, I've got a session shortly, so we need to head to the recreation room."

Wait, is that it? I deliberated, confused. *No punishment for what I did?* I presumed he had forgotten, and I had no intention of reminding him.

I quietly followed Doctor Hailey out of his office, and he grabbed my arm as soon as he had locked the door; it was surprisingly gentle, considering I was apparently a patient. We then headed back down the stairwell, passed solitary confinement, all the way to where the incident with the German doctor had occurred. I then noticed the reception area was now empty except for the receptionist. *I could make a run for it.* I contemplated as Doctor Hailey hardly had a hold on me; I also didn't know when I would get another opportunity. *It could be now or never.*

Just as I readied myself to bolt, Doctor Hailey unexpectedly tugged me left down a white-walled corridor where my shoes squeaked against the hardwood floor; it was directly opposite the reception area. ***NO!*** I wanted to scream in frustration as it felt, yet again, that freedom had slipped through my grasp. *I should've run! I should've just fucking run for it!* Now I had no choice but to behave as orderlies patrolled this seemingly interminable corridor; there was no end in sight as far as the eye could see.

"I'll inform you when your next session with Fred is." Doctor Hailey said in a hushed tone before tugging me right into a large, stark white, windowless hall with a stage along the back. Recreational items like a TV, record player and sofa were located towards the back beneath the stage. *Holy... Fucking... Shit...* I was at a loss for words when I stared around in disbelief, taking in the patients dressed in the same garb as me. *This... This can't be real!* Just seeing all of them was like a smack to the face. I was still yet to awake from this nightmare, making me wonder whether this was actually my reality. *Was Travis just a figment of my imagination all along?*

Doctor Hailey pushed me further into the room, the hardwood floor continuing from the hallway. *Where's he taking me?* I wondered, now realising he was herding me towards a circular table with a spare seat. Other patients were also sat at tables scattered around the hall, reminding me of a school canteen. Then I spotted orderlies pushing catering trollies while nurses handed out trays to the patients. Occasionally, the orderlies would disappear through a door along the left-hand wall when the trollies were empty.

*This **must** be a dream.* But it felt all too real, especially when I was shoved down onto a hard, plastic chair. *Please, just wake up!* I begged as a tray was deposited in front of me. A glob of beige that had the consistency of phlegm jiggled, making me grimace at whatever the hell it was. *Is this meant to be foo-* **THUD!** A jug of water was then haphazardly put on the table, most splashing out over the rim. Glancing up, I only noticed the nurse as she turned back for the catering trolley, grabbing tiny paper pots that she set down next to each patient. *What the?* Peering inside, I saw a kaleidoscope of colours that I soon grasped were pills.

Unexpectedly, a hand rested on my shoulder, and I spotted a tarnished gold wedding band. I noted it was Doctor Hailey when he leaned down beside me.

"Just keep doing what you're doing." He whispered in my ear, grabbing the pot of pills when the nurse had turned back for the trolley.

I had to do a doubletake. *Hang on, what's he doing?* I incredulously watched as he emptied the pills into his white coat, discarding the pot back on the table. *Did he do what I just think he did?...*

I barely had time to register what had happened before Doctor Hailey rose to his feet, growling down at me in a shockingly glottal tone, "I don't expect you to act out of line again! Otherwise, there shall be dire consequences!" And, without another word, he left.

What the fuck was all that about? I pondered, staring after him. *And what do I do now?*

"You're looking rather... Tasty today..." A hoarse voice spoke up, distracting me.

Only now did I notice the other seven patients sitting around the table, but I locked eyes with the one directly opposite me with white, bristly hair. *What did he just say?* I opened my mouth to ask but realised I didn't want to talk to him.

There was something cold about this guy, something inhuman that made my instincts scream to run. I didn't know if it had anything to do with his frosty blue eyes set into his craggy face or the sanguineous smirk that hooked his thin lips. Either way, I hastily averted my gaze to the glob on the tray. *I was probably hearing things, anyway...* I tried to reassure myself. *He's probably just talking about this food, trying to be funny or something...* But I could feel him still staring, his eyes practically burning a hole through me.

Apprehensively peering back up, I noted his expression hadn't changed. It was rather chilling, like staring at a real-life mannequin. *Maybe he wants my food?*

Slowly pushing the tray over to him, I offered with a weak smile, "Here, you have it."

I didn't get the chance to pull my hand back before he lunged over the table, snatching my wrist with his excruciatingly tight grasp.

"What are you doing?! **LET ME GO!**" I hawked, trying to pull my hand free, but he managed to yank me halfway across the table, causing the jug of water to spill everywhere.

"Ah-ah-aaahhhh!" A nurse appeared, scolding my captor as if he were a dog, "Leave him!"

His frosty blue eyes shifted from the nurse, back to me, before he reluctantly released me. Swiftly scurrying off the table, I pressed my hand to my chest, feeling the phlegmy glob that had splattered all down me, but that was the least of my worries. *Why the hell did that guy grab me?!*

"What have we told you?!" The nurse continued to reprimand the patient, wagging her index finger, "You're **not** to behave like a Neander-"

Unexpectedly, he snatched her by the wrist, yanking her towards him and biting down on her arm. A harrowing scream erupted from her like a banshee in the dead of night. *Holy fuck!* I gaped at the bloody carnage just as orderlies rushed over. I immediately jumped to my feet when the table went flying; the patient now tackled to the floor.

Did that really just happen?! I stupidly questioned, but it just felt too surreal to be absolute. Even watching the patient being dragged away towards the long corridor, with his gore-riddled face reminding me so much of that man in The Silence of the Lambs, I still found it hard to comprehend.

A high-pitched alarm then resounded throughout the asylum, similar to a bird or whistle but far less harmonic; it was so loud I wouldn't have been surprised if my ears were bleeding. Doctors had now appeared, all honing in on the nurse bleeding on the floor. But what piqued my interest was the orderlies and nurses trying to keep the patients at bay, ushering them towards the recreational items at the back of the room.

I knew now was my chance to escape, so I made sure no one was looking when I made a dash for the long corridor. *Please be empty!* I carefully peered right to ensure no one was patrolling, relieved the hallway was dead. *Thank God!* I breathed, glimpsing left in the direction of the reception, only to jump back with a fright when I came face-to-face with a dark-haired young man I didn't recognise.

Holy fuck! I panicked, glancing up at him and realising he was an inch or so taller than me. *Who is this guy?* I already figured he was a patient by the uniform. Then I clocked his arms; they looked like they had seen better days as they were marred with scars. *Why's he just staring at me?* His hazel-coloured eyes bore into mine expectantly, like a dog waiting for a bone. He even had that innocent yet excited vibe about him as he shifted from foot to foot, causing his curly hair to bounce.

Just as I was about to tell him to go away, he frantically waved his hand in front of my face, loudly exclaiming, "**Hey, Ricky!**"

I couldn't help but flinch in fear someone may have heard him. *What the fuck's he doing?!* I fumed, pressing a finger to my lips, an evident gesture to be quiet.

He clearly didn't understand and noisily carried on, "Whatcya doing?! Whereya going?! Whoya seeing?!" His annoying, singsong voice instantly rubbed me up the wrong way.

Seriously, who the fuck is this guy?!

"What the fuck you doing?!" I snapped, and he instantly corrected me, "What the fuck **are** you doing?"

Is this guy for real?!

Clenching my jaw, I growled through gritted teeth, "Just go the fuck aw-" But the clip-clop of heels distracted me.

Glancing beyond him towards the reception, I saw a handful of oblivious nurses cackling like a brood of hens. *Shit!* I had no choice but to retreat into the recreation room. Whoever this guy was followed me like a lost puppy. *Fuck it! There goes my chance of getting outta here!*

Everyone was still distracted by the nurse on the floor, and hope of escape swiftly returned. *I could slip through there...* I contemplated, peering over at the door along the left-hand wall. I had no idea where it led, but **now** was my chance. *And I'll be damned if this guy fucks it up!*

Shooting him a warning glance, I stated, "I'll be back in a minute." But I had no intention of returning; I just wanted him to leave me alone.

I then sprinted for the door, which opened with a creak. A sigh of relief escaped me when I peeked inside; the white, windowless room was empty. My shoes squeaked against the hardwood floor when I stepped inside, glimpsing at the dirty plates piled on the wooden counter along the right-hand wall.

What is this room? Matching cabinets were stationed above, and clean dishes, bowls and cups were stored inside. *Is this some kind of service room?* I pondered further, my attention shifting to the catering trollies lined up along the left wall.

I then hurried towards the door directly opposite at the far end, making sure to be as quiet as a mouse, but I may as well not have bothered as the door behind swung open with a bang. My head snapped over my shoulder, only to see that guy standing there with a delightful grin gracing his sculpted face.
Why the hell's he following me?!

I didn't get the chance to interrogate him as he swiftly exclaimed, "You were longer than a minute!"
Is he fucking serious?! I gaped, unable to do anything but slowly blink at him in stunned silence.
"So, I thought I'd come and find you." He blissfully carried on just as the door slammed shut behind him, "After all, that's what the bestest of best buds do, right?" I was immediately brought up short by that last comment.
Wait, best buds? I wanted to laugh but was too shocked by the events rapidly unravelling. *Right now, I don't care; I just need to get outta here!* Albeit with my '**best bud**'.

Without shooting him another glance, I turned back for the door at the far end, secretly hoping he would get the hint to leave me alone. *But I very much doubt it...* Opening the door, I gazed inside, realising it led to a commercial kitchen. *There must be a way out of here!* Stepping inside, I hurriedly peered around before the door behind me opened, my heart dropping as I knew that annoying guy had followed. *I need to lose him.* I realised before spotting two doors along the back wall.

"Where were you last night?" He asked as I bypassed the stainless-steel cookers in the middle of the room, making a beeline for the back of the kitchen, "You said you'd teach me poker."
I didn't have the time or patience for his insistent questioning, so I growled over my shoulder, "Look, I'll teach you tonight, okay?! Now go away!"

He hadn't listened as he wondered, "What are we doing here?"
Spinning round to face him where we came nose to nose, I spat, "Seriously, why the fuck are you following me?!"
"Be... Because we're the bestest of best buds, Ricky-"

"Stop calling me Ricky!" I heatedly intervened, "My name's **not**-"

"Ricky?" A silvery voice piped up.

Turning around, a female patient with long, wavy blonde hair emerged from the right-hand door along the back. *Whoa!* I had to do a doubletake when she stepped closer. She could easily have been Harper's older sister if she had one. *Albeit a mean-looking sister...* I put that down to the left side of her head being shaved, the hairline braided so it swept over to the right. *Who is she?* I pondered when she took another purposeful step closer, and I now towered over her. Her sky-blue eyes peered up at me, so lifeless I would have thought they belonged to a corpse if she weren't standing before me.

"You never mentioned **he** would be joining us..." She murmured, gesturing with a nod towards the annoying guy beside me.

Then I clocked the scar on the shaved side of her head, curving from her ear to the base of her neck. *How did she get that?* But then I realised what she had said. *Wait, '**joining**' us?* I couldn't help but stare between them, wondering if she was suggesting what I thought she was. *Ergh, God, no!*

"Look, Ricky." The woman sharply spoke up, folding her arms across her chest, "I ain't got a clue what the fuck you're playing at, but you said you wanted to talk, so talk."

"'**Ain't**' isn't a word." The annoying guy corrected before turning to me, adding, "Thinking about it, you also said you wanted to talk to me about something."

The excitement plastered across his beaming face was like a kid on Christmas Eve, "What was it? Was it the same thing?"

I had no idea what either of them were talking about. *What the fuck is going-* The door to the service room abruptly swung open, and we all snapped our heads over to see an orderly standing in the doorway. *Fuck!* I panicked, frozen like a deer caught in the headlights.

"Hey, what are you three doing in here?!" The orderly squawked before hollering over his shoulder, "**THERE'S THREE PATIENTS IN HERE!**"

Chapter Four

It was just a dream...

"Richard, Richard, Richard..." Doctor Sasin muttered, slowly shaking his head whilst pacing behind his desk, causing the smoke from his cigarette to part for him like the Red Sea.

I was strapped to the gas chamber-looking chair; the presence of Nurse Deadman and the two orderlies lingered behind me like a bad smell.

"What happened, Richard?" Doctor Sasin queried before stubbing out his cigarette, no longer pacing when his glacial blue eyes locked onto me, "Why did you attack Doctor Kröger? And why were you found in the kitchen with two other patients?"

It took every ounce of self-control to not snap at him for calling me Richard. *I'm getting pretty sick of it!* Instead, I stared at him, refusing to reply as I knew it would only lead to regret.

After a moment of silence, Doctor Sasin spoke more to himself, "I've got no other choice but to try an alternative treatment."

What alternative treatment? I worried, wanting to bring my hands up to rub my face, but I couldn't.

"Metrazol therapy should do the tri-"

"Metrazol therapy?!" I intervened in a slightly high-pitched tone, shocked.

No, that's illegal! I assured myself, remembering I had used various psychiatric hospitals as part of my major project for the Investigation, Documentary and Innovation module at university.

"You're joking, right?!" I blurted, taking Doctor Sasin aback, who was now sitting behind his desk.

"Why would I be joking?" He curiously wondered, so I swiftly countered, "Metrazol therapy was discontinued back in the 40's because of the high fatality rate!"

"Ah, so you're not as stupid as you look." He mocked, "Yes. Unfortunately, it was discontinued thirty-odd years ago."

Wait, did he say thirty years ago? I quickly counted in my head. *No, it was banned sixty years ago... What the fuck is wrong with this guy?*

"But why fix or change something that isn't broken?" Doctor Sasin continued with a bloodcurdling smirk, trying to intimidate me.

"Because of the **high** fatality rate!" I pointed out, tension lacing my voice as my throat felt like it was closing up.

Slowly, his smirk vanished, and that straight face I was so used to had returned.

"My patients only die if I want them to." He retorted, and I couldn't stop a shudder creeping up my spine from that sentence alone.

Doctor Sasin then snapped his attention to Nurse Deadman, who was still behind me.

"Take Mr Moon to the therapy room." He commanded.

"But Doctor Scandura has booked the treatment room for today." Nurse Deadman pointed out once she came to stand beside me.

"Do I need to remind you whose hospital this is?!" He scolded her sharply, and I remembered Doctor Hailey had said something similar earlier that day.

'***You fail to remember that this is my hospital.***'*. Does that mean they are both owners?*

When Nurse Deadman didn't reply, Doctor Sasin impatiently growled, "Just take him to the therapy room as I told you!" He folded his arms over his chest before continuing, "I'll be along shortly once I have called Tobias, so make sure everything is ready when I get there."

He then ushered us to leave with a sharp wave of his hand when the orderlies unfastened the straps, hoisting me to my feet.

"No, no, no, you can't do this!" I panicked, a sickening sensation rolling in my gut at the thought of what would soon happen to me.

"Yes, I can..." Doctor Sasin murmured, not once looking over as I was dragged out of his office.

"IT'S ILLEGAL!" I hollered, but Nurse Deadman had slammed the door, so I desperately tried to break free from the orderlies hold.

*He **can't** do this!*

"PLEASE!" I screamed uncontrollably when we reached the stairwell, but neither Nurse Deadman nor the orderlies reacted to my hysterics.

"**PLEASE!**" I begged again as I was dragged down the steps, my hands clenching into fists when my heart rate kicked up a notch, so fast it felt like I couldn't breathe.

Nurse Deadman's blue eyes locked onto mine when she held the door open at the bottom; I knew now was my chance to try and get through to her.

"You **know** this is illegal!" I assured, my breath temporarily bottling up in my chest in anticipation.

Her infamous reptilian smile hooked her lips as she replied, "And you know that doesn't change anything."

All hope was then immediately dashed from me. *No, no, no, this can't be happening! PLEASE JUST WAKE UP!*

The orderlies then yanked me down the corridor directly ahead, sunlight pooling in from the massive window along the left. It didn't take long for me to recognise where I was. *NO!* I panicked just as the door to the hydrotherapy room loomed up ahead. *I've got to get outta here!* But it didn't matter how hard I fought against the orderlies; I was no match for them.

"Please, don't do this!" I pleaded when Nurse Deadman opened a different door to a small, dilapidated room.

I vaguely noticed the top half of the walls were off-white, while the bottom was covered in mint green tiles.

"I promise I won't press any charges if you just let me go!" I desperately carried on but was ignored yet again, so I snatched hold of the doorframe when the orderlies went to drag me inside.

"Just let go, Mr Moon..." Nurse Deadman uttered with a slight sneer, stepping inside and folding her arms across her chest, "You're only preventing the inevitable."

I didn't get the chance to react – *Not that I would have let go, anyway* – before the orderlies yanked me free with such ferocity a few of my nails were ripped from their nail beds, making me cry out in agony.

"Stop your whining!" Nurse Deadman scolded, gaining my attention when she gestured to a bed in the middle of the room, the head towards the right wall.
An overpowering sense of dread consumed me, my eyes darting around in search of an alternate escape route, but all I could focus on was the large, invasive-looking light that hung above the bed; ECT equipment was beside it on a trolley. *How am I gonna get out of here?!*

"Strap him down." Nurse Deadman commanded, and I immediately screamed, "NO!"
I lashed out for the first thing I could get my hands on while being dragged further inside, my heels digging into the off-brown, lino flooring to no avail. Grabbing something metal, I thought it would be sturdy; however, it was a trolley with wheels and ended up coming with us.
"**PLUH-PLEASE!**" I sobbed, my chest so tight it felt like I was suffocating, "**LUH-LET ME GUH-GO!**"

The orderlies merely hauled me over to the bed as if I weighed nothing, throwing me down where I realised it had recently been used as it was still warm. They couldn't fasten the straps quickly enough as I thrashed my limbs whenever they tried to pin me down.

"Oh for Pete's sake!" Nurse Deadman seethed before the clip of her heels advanced on us, "Both of you hold him still, and I'll secure the straps!"
She then appeared alongside the bed just as the orderlies each held down two of my limbs, their fingers biting into my flesh.

"Please, just let me go!" I begged as she securely fastened a strap over my biceps and chest, moving onto the cuffs for my wrists and ankles.
Once she had finished, Nurse Deadman stared down at me with her stone-cold, blue eyes before sauntering off towards a tall, green cabinet in the far left-hand corner.

This can't be real! I fretted, my breaths becoming quick and shallow. *This **can't** be real!* Sweat now profusely seeped through my clothes, my heart beating so hard I wouldn't have been surprised if I were having a heart attack. Closing my eyes, I prayed. *Please, just wake-* **BANG!** Startled, I anxiously peered toward the door where Doctor Sasin had now appeared, making my heart plummet. *Oh God, no! **Please**, wake up!* I struggled against my restraints, hoping they would loosen.

"Right, Richard." Doctor Sasin began, now standing beside me on my left, "Seeing as you're an '**expert**' in Metrazol therapy, I don't need to tell you what's going to happen."
He rolled up the sleeves of his long, white coat just as Nurse Deadman appeared with a trolley at the foot of the bed.

"You can't fucking do this!" I reiterated before he produced a needle from the trolley, making me tremble as dread set in once more.

Please, someone – anyone - help me! I prayed I would be rescued, but deep down, I knew no one would come for me. All I could do was watch as Doctor Sasin flicked the end of the needle, causing some liquid to spurt from the tip. That was when I began to imagine my worst-case scenario. *I'm gonna die!* The next thought made an ache form in the back of my throat. *Harper's gonna think I left her, abandoned her and the kids! Our baby's gonna grow up without a father!*

A sanguineous smirk then hooked Doctor Sasin's lips when he mocked, "I can do whatever the fuck I like in **my** hospital."
He bent down to inject the needle into my left arm just as a sudden, unexpected wave of determination flooded throughout me. *Not if I can fucking help it!*
When his face was uncomfortably close to mine, I declared in a low baritone, "Over my dead fucking body!" And I abruptly leant up, headbutting him with such unrelenting force he staggered backwards with a groan.

One of the orderlies managed to steady Doctor Sasin before he tumbled into the wall, but the needle fell from his grasp, smashing against the floor.

"Oh my word!" Nurse Deadman gasped, slapping a hand over her gaping mouth, "Fred, are you okay?!"
She hurried over just as both orderlies turned to me; I didn't need to be a psychic to know what would happen next.

BANG! One ruthlessly punched me in the gut, knocking the wind right out of me. I just lay there gasping for air, trying to ignore the nauseating wave that crashed over me when it felt as if my organs had been rearranged. I barely had a chance to regain myself when the other cracked his knuckles clean across my face, instantly making my eyes and nose water; the tang of copper now lingered on my tongue. It was a smack to my pride I hadn't even known I was suppressing, but I merely put it down to the fact I couldn't even fight back like a man.

"That's enough!" Doctor Sasin sharply intervened when the orderlies raised their fists once more, making a sigh of relief escape me.

They then stepped away, and Doctor Sasin came to stand beside me again. He was dabbing a bloodstained tissue against his nose, making me realise I must have given him a nosebleed. *Good!*

"Deadman," He began, passing her the tissue, "Prepare 70mg of curare." Then his attention shifted to the orderlies, "Hold him still this time."

I immediately tensed when one dug the heel of his palms into my shoulders; the other pressed a hand to my forehead using most of his weight.

"**THIS IS FUCKING ILLEGAL!**" I screamed in a high-pitched tone, squirming in the hopes it would somehow loosen the straps and I could make a run for it.

Smirking maniacally down at me, Doctor Sasin said, "Not if no one knows about it."

He roughly yanked my left arm down, jabbing the needle into the crease of my elbow, steadily pushing the syringe for what felt like an eternity when, in reality, it was barely even a minute. I wasn't a crier; I could probably count the number of times I had cried on one hand, but that was all I wanted to do as I felt my body grow weaker, almost impaired.

By now, Doctor Sasin had unfastened the restraints, but I couldn't move; I could hardly see as my eyes grew heavy. He then began lifting my arms, dropping them without care by my sides before moving onto my legs, repeating the same process. Occasionally, with great difficulty, I could move my head, but only from side to side. Being awake but not in control of my body was genuinely terrifying. *Please be a nightmare!* ***Please*** *be a nightmare!*

I was then vaguely aware when Doctor Sasin injected me with another needle, crossing my arms over my chest once he was done. That was when the convulsions started. My mouth opened and closed of its own accord, my limbs jerking as flashing lights danced in my eyes before everything went black.

A gasp erupted out of me as I sat bolt upright, staring around the darkened room. *Where am I?!* I panicked before a hand grasped my bicep, making me scream in fright as I flinched away.

"Hey, hey, it's okay!" A soft, feminine voice cooed, "It's okay! You're okay!"

Harper?! My mouth slackened in disbelief before I automatically reached for the bedside lamp, turning it on with a click. To my surprise and relief, she was sat up in bed wearing a light blue vest, her long, startling blonde hair tumbling down her shoulders in waves. *Oh my God, it was just a dream!* Slumping back onto my pillow, I breathed in the familiar aroma of that awful kebab shop below. *It was just a dream...*

"You going to tell me what all that was about?" Harper pried as she leaned on her elbows, staring down at me with quizzical green eyes.

Part of me didn't want to. *I don't want to think about it ever again!* But I also needed to tell someone, to air my feelings that the dream had engraved deep within me.

Gripping my hands together, I repeatedly pinched the skin between my thumb and forefinger while replying in a strained tone, "I... I just had the craziest dream..."

"It sounded more like a nightmare than a dream." Harper pointed out.

I merely shot her an unimpressed look before telling her everything that had happened.

"And they didn't believe you weren't a patient?" She asked after a moment of silence, curiously carrying on when I nodded, "Why? What did you apparently do?"

Shaking my head, I closed my eyes and reluctantly responded, "No idea, but everyone kept thinking I was someone else."

"Who?" Harper wondered, intrigued, "Who did they think you were?"

I didn't get the chance to reply as a hoarse, masculine voice answered for me, "Richard Moon."

What the?! My eyes snapped open, and a terrified scream escaped me when I saw Doctor Sasin leering over me. *WHAT THE FUCK?!*

Unexpectedly, I was plunged back into darkness, abruptly sitting bolt upright with another gasp. Slowly, my eyes adjusted, and a realisation dawned on me as I gazed around the tiny, fully tiled white room. *No!* I declared in disbelief, staggering to my feet only to fall back onto the hard bed; I didn't have the strength to stand. *NO!* There was no doubt I was in solitary confinement. That was when the disbelief vanished, replaced with despair.

Tipping my head back, I let it flop forward as an uncontrollable cry escaped my hold, "**NOOOO!**"

Chapter Five

Who the fuck's Jack and Adi?!

CLONK! A key turned in the lock, startling me. *Urgh...* I groaned, the noise amplifying the headache pounding away, so I pinched the bridge of my nose in the hopes it would alleviate the pain.

I lay on the cold, hard bed, staring groggily up at the darkened ceiling for what felt like hours, unable to sleep as I wasn't willing to endure that heartache again. *I thought it was over... That I was back to my normal life...*

The door then opened, bathing the cell with some much-needed light; I had to shield my eyes as it was blinding.

"Get up!" A venomous voice spat; I didn't need to look at them to know it was Nurse Deadman.

"It's time for a shower." She added, my eyes slowly adjusting and making out her blue ones staring down at me.

A shower? I repeated, my body aching just lying down, never mind standing up.

When I didn't move, Nurse Deadman's voice cracked through the cell like a chain whip, "GET UP!" And I instantly flinched out of pure shock.

She then turned to someone beside her before I could respond.

"Get him out." She instructed, and two strong hands reached inside, grasping me by the front of my shirt.

I realised it was the two orderlies who seemed to follow her around like lost puppies.

I barely had the chance to regain my balance before I was dragged down the corridor towards the gated entrance.

What are they gonna do with me today?! I fretted while Nurse Deadman spoke to the stationed guard. *I can't go through all that again!* I bit my bottom lip at the thought of that horrid treatment.

Once we were allowed through, Nurse Deadman led the way and turned left. I immediately recognised where we were; the gated door just up ahead led to the reception area. However, we soon stopped by another with a stationed guard on our left. *Wait, where are we going?* I worried, confused, as I couldn't recall seeing this passageway yesterday. *Then again, I was more preoccupied with how I was gonna get out of here.* Today, I didn't have the energy or the mental strength to fight.

To my surprise, the guard didn't ask any questions and merely granted us access. *Is this where the showers are?* I wondered while Nurse Deadman led the way down the cream-walled hallway, the rap of her shoes echoed along the hardwood floor.

Unexpectedly, she came to an abrupt halt, an oof escaping me when I was pulled to a stop next to an arch on my right. I could hear an array of noises, from maniacal laughter to shrill screams that stabbed my brain like a thousand shards of glass. *God, my head...* I inwardly groaned, wanting to bring my left hand up to pinch my nose, but the orderlies hold on me was unyielding.

"Tim, Tom," Nurse Deadman began, gaining their attention, "Take Mr Moon inside for his shower. Once he is done, escort him to the recreation room." A hungry grin spread across her face when she said, "I'll be with Fred if you need me." And, without another word, she turned back for the gated entrance and left.

Suddenly, I was yanked inside, my shoes slapping against the concrete floor before I was pulled to a standstill. Peering around in dismay, I watched orderlies drag naked patients between this room and another through an archway to my right. *I guess this must be the changing room.* I deliberated when I spotted clothes hanging on hooks along the concrete wall.

"Hurry up and get undressed." One of the orderlies instructed; I didn't know whether he was Tim or Tom, but I had dubbed him Schwarzenegger.
He then shoved me towards an empty hook along the back wall.

I really don't wanna do this... I uttered, my chest tightening as I knew I had no choice but to obey. I wasn't the type of person to be uncomfortable in my skin, but being forced to strip with no means of dignity whatsoever was a newfound low.

Once I had reluctantly hung my clothes up, I was ushered through the archway only to realise the newfound low I had experienced moments ago was now a thing of the past. *Oh my fucking God!* I gaped, unsure what to process first as I stared from the shower heads fixed to the left wall to the line of toilets on my right. *There're no privacy walls, curtains, nothing!* I had expected that for the showers. *But not the toilets!* However, I was soon distracted by the naked patients running amok. Some laughed hysterically, while others screamed at the top of their lungs. *Wait, is that guy bashing his head against the wall?* An orderly then pulled him away, and I spotted a trickle of blood drip down his face, confirming my suspicions.

"Don't just stand there!" The orderly I had nicknamed Stallone growled, "Go and use the fucking shower!"
Honestly, I don't want to. Especially when the majority of patients were charging around like horses at the Grand National. *But it's not like I've got a choice...* I hesitantly wandered over to the shower away from everybody else, acutely aware of the cold water splashing underfoot. Turning the taps, I was horrified when freezing water crashed over me. *FUCK!* I involuntarily gasped, briskly washing before heading back into the changing room, pulling on my clothes so fast I could have sworn I gave myself friction burns.

Once I was dressed, the orderlies escorted me to the recreation room as breakfast was being served. Much to my disappointment, I was sat at the same table as yesterday. *With the same guy sat opposite me...* He had that sanguineous smirk on his craggy face, his frosty blue eyes practically burning a hole through me. *What the fuck is wrong with this guy?* I wondered just as a tray was set down in front of me; I couldn't help but grimace at the glob. *Is this all they feed us? Something that looks like phlegm?*

"You're looking rather... Tasty today..." That strange patient spoke up in a hoarse voice, gaining my attention.
Why does he keep saying that? I deliberated with a furrowed brow. *And why's he just staring at me?* The murderous, hungry

look in his chilling gaze would put a wolf to shame; it honestly made me feel like a lamb to slaughter.

I was gladly distracted when a nurse placed a tiny paper pot beside my tray. Peering down, I noted it was filled with pills in a kaleidoscope of colours. *What are these?*

Curiosity got the better of me, and I glanced up at the nurse, querying, "What are these?"

"They're tablets." She replied in a condescending tone, so I heatedly retorted, "Yeah, I can see that, but **what** are they?!"

Narrowing her eyes, she pursed her lips together before raising her voice like I were a disobedient child, "Just take your goddamn tablets, Richard!"

"Everything alright over here?" A masculine voice piped up before the thud of footsteps advanced on us.

Glimpsing over my shoulder, an orderly now towered over me, and I wondered whether this asylum had hired famous Hollywood actors. *He could easily be Jason Statham's stunt double!* But I realised that was the least of my worries when he stared threateningly down at me. *Is he trying to intimidate me?!* My muscles quivered when he folded his hulking arms across his chest, oozing male bravado as if it were cologne.

His attitude didn't sway me easily; I merely shifted my attention back to the nurse, stating, "I'm not taking them until I know what they are." My response initiated a crack of knuckles from Statham.

"Take them, or I'll **make** you." He bullied.

Raising my right eyebrow in disbelief, I scoffed, "Make me then-"

"Leave it with me, Jay." An articulate voice swiftly interrupted, "I'll see to it that Rick takes his pills."

Doctor Hailey appeared beside us, grabbing the pill pot in question.

What's he doing her- Unexpectedly, he snatched me up by my shirt collar before I could even finish that thought.

"I've had just about enough of your antics, Mr Moon!" He snapped, roughly shunting me toward the hallway before I barely had the chance to gain my balance.

"What are you doing?!" I fumed, trying to shake off his hold to no avail.

Doctor Hailey said nothing as he pushed me out of the recreation room.

Where the hell is he taking me?! I worried when we headed right down the corridor. I opened my mouth to ask, but an oof came out when he forced me against the left-hand wall beside a door, spinning me around and grasping me by the front of my shirt.

"What the fuck happened yesterday?!" He barked in a whisper, his face so close to mine I could feel his hot breath beat against me.

What the hell is he on about?

"Erm..." I murmured in uncertainty, "What do you mean?"

"You weren't scheduled for a therapy session yesterday!" He quietly yelled, scrunching up the pill pot and shoving it into his coat pocket, "But you clearly pissed Fred off!"

Inhaling a steady breath, Doctor Hailey carried on in a hushed tone, "At least you-"

BANG! The door beside us swung open, stopping him mid-sentence when an orderly stepped out. Their eyes locked briefly before they exchanged polite nods, and the orderly disappeared toward the entrance block.

"As I was saying," Doctor Hailey continued, his dark, penetrating gaze shifting back to me, "At least you got the evidence we needed." And a smile of relief graced his hatchet face.

Again with the evidence... I still had no idea what he was talking about, and I guessed it showed by the bafflement on my face as his smile swiftly vanished.

"You did get the evidence, didn't you?" Doctor Hailey sceptically asked, "You were wearing the camera, weren't you?"

"Camera?" I absentmindedly blurted before he banged a fist against the wall beside my head, making me flinch out of both shock and fright.

"Oh for fuck's sake!" He fumed, his face reddening by the second, "You didn't think to put your fucking camera on?!"

I thought he was going to punch me, but he abruptly turned away, burying his head in his hands.

What the hell is going on? I deliberated, watching Doctor Hailey pace up and down. *What evidence? What camera?* I didn't have time to dwell on those thoughts as he swiftly lowered his hands, turning back to face me.

"Please tell me you've at least spoken to Jack and Adi!" He urged in a quieter tone, and I was now even more confused.

Wait, what, who?! I exclaimed, my head flinching back slightly. *Who the fuck's Jack and Adi?!* My silence must have been a dead giveaway as a frustrated growl seeped from Doctor Hailey's lips.

"Why not?!" He demanded through gritted teeth just before a nurse emerged from the recreation room, her entire features seeming to light up when her eyes landed on him. "Great..." He uttered under his breath when she headed in our direction, but that frown on his face swiftly vanished when she was a stone's throw away.

He hastily covered his left hand with his right when she grinned at him, "Morning, Elon."

A blush crept along her cheeks when he replied, "Morning, Evelyn."

I could have sworn I heard a longing sigh seep from her lips as she wandered down the hallway. *How can she be interested in **him**?* I thought with a suspicious raise of my brow, momentarily staring Doctor Hailey up and down. He was the iconic vision of any movie villain, especially with that scar zigzagging down his face.

"Why?" Doctor Hailey pressed once the nurse was no longer in sight, his hands now clenched by his sides.

I didn't know what to say that would pacify him. *I don't even know what the hell's going on! Evidence? Camera? Jack and Adi? What the fuck?*

However, I knew I needed to say something, so I explained, "I was in solitary confinement."

"What?" He queried in disbelief, lifting a single eyebrow and cocking his head, "Again?"

"Yeah, last night." I confirmed, riling him up by the audible sound of his teeth grinding.

After a few steady breaths, Doctor Hailey uttered, "Well, it is what it is... But, **please**, talk to them today. We're running out of time."

I suddenly felt a wave of coldness crash over me as everything became overwhelming. *Wait, running out of time?!* I echoed. *Out of time for what?!* But I couldn't ask; he already seemed suspicious of my behaviour.

"In the meantime," Doctor Hailey added, herding me back toward the recreation room, "I'll find out when your next session with Fred is."

Wait, what the hell am I meant to be doing?! And how the hell am I meant to figure out who Jack and Adi are?! But I kept my mouth shut despite the gnawing sensation to question him becoming almost unbearable.

Once we reached the table, I spotted my breakfast unfortunately still there.

"If I have to have words with you again about taking your pills, Mr Moon, then there'll be serious consequences!" Doctor Hailey threatened.

He then forcefully sat me down, causing the chair legs to creak in protest. *I swear he's like Doctor Jekyll and Mr Hyde...* I murmured when he left without another word.

After the disgusting breakfast, orderlies tidied the tables while nurses guided patients to the recreational items by the stage. The record player, next to the steps leading up to the stage, was a firm favourite as a handful of patients were gathered around shrieking at one another. *I'm guessing they can't decide on the music...* I mulled, watching in amusement as a nurse tried to calm the situation, but they weren't listening to her.

THUD! Peering over to my left, I spotted a bookshelf against the wall with a smattering of hard-looking chairs in front of it. **THUD!** A giggling patient pulled books off one by one, letting them fall to the floor. **THUD!** *How annoying...* I griped, noting a few patients trying to read looked visibly irritated.

I had no idea what to do with myself, but the incessant, blood-chilling screams and irrepressible laughter were too much; I couldn't think clearly as they crashed over me like a tsunami. **THUD!** The books still being pulled off the shelf were like timpani drums over the ruthless waves of noise.

Fuck this! I growled, unable to deal with being in this asylum a moment longer. *I need to get outta here!* Bypassing the two tatty sofas that faced one another, I made a beeline for the stage steps. *There must be an exit or something up there.* I hoped just before the crackling of the record player came to life. I was pleasantly surprised by the upbeat guitar strings that resounded throughout the room, followed by a deep timbre. '**We're caught in a traap, I can't waaaalk ouut, because I looove you too much, baabbbyyy.**'. It was soon in competition with the TV along the right-hand wall; a handful of chairs were scattered around it.

When the steps were just out of reach, someone unexpectedly jumped in front of me.

"ARGGH!" I screamed, recoiling before realising who it was. *What does he want?!* I immediately pressed my lips together as frustration set in.

Throwing his arms up into the air as if to pull me into a hug, that annoying patient exclaimed, "Riiiiickyyyyyyy!"

It took every ounce of self-control to stop myself from snapping.

"Whatcya doing?! Whereya going?! Whoya seeing?!" He blissfully carried on whilst I glowered at him.

Oh my fucking God... I wanted to scream. I wanted to fist my hair. But I just found myself staring at him in disbelief when I realised. *He's not gonna leave me alone...*

"You didn't teach me poker last night..." He pouted, wrapping his arms around his body to hug himself whilst twisting from side to side.

Urgh... I inwardly groaned, shaking my head. *Perhaps he'll leave me alone if I teach him...* I glimpsed over at the unoccupied sofas, the wooden table in-between scattered with cards. *I can't believe I'm doing this...*

"Fine." I griped, drawing in a breath before releasing it, "I'll show you now."

I didn't wait for him to respond before advancing on the sofas, sitting down on the one that faced the bookshelf.

An ensemble of enthusiastic noises escaped him as he skipped over, plonking himself down opposite whilst I gathered the cards, shuffling them.

"I'm super-duper excited!" He proclaimed, clapping his hands together like a baby that had figured it out for the first time.

Is this guy for real?... I muttered, staring at him through my dishevelled hair that hung in my face. *He's acting like a child!* But then I realised where I was. *What am I thinking?... Of course this guy's for real... There's obviously something wrong with him...*

"Sooo..." He began when I fixed my attention back down to the cards, dealing him two, "What happened to you yesterday after they caught us in the kitchen?"

What did happen? I mulled for a split second before remembering. *Metrazol therapy...* I couldn't stop the shudder that swept throughout my body as I vividly recollected every moment. The maniacal smirk on Doctor Sasin's lips as he leered over me. The sharp scratch when he roughly jabbed the needle into my arm. My lifeless body then his to abuse.

Blood pounded in my ears as rage rapidly consumed me. The effects of Doctor Sasin's actions still lingered, igniting something feral within me. ***IT WAS FUCKING ILLEGAL WHAT HE DID!*** Yet, he would never suffer the consequences of his actions. *He's gonna regret-* **SNAP! SNAP!** The click of fingers dragged me out of my unspoken animosity. Blinking, I soon realised it was that annoying patient trying to get my attention.

"Ricky?" **CLICK!** "Ricky?" **CLICK!** "Ricky?" He repeated over and over, "Ricky?" **CLICK!** "Rick-"

"**What?!**" I heatedly snapped, taking him aback.

"Is... Is everything okay?" He hesitantly queried, "You dropped the cards and just stared at nothing."

What? Peering down, I noticed the cards scattered by my feet and quickly scooped them up.

"I'm fine." I replied a little too readily, "Just got a lot on my mind."

Like how I'm gonna get out of here. Then there's all that weird stuff about evidence that doctor keeps going on about. Evidence for what? And he said I have a camera, but where?

Then Doctor Hailey's other comment sprung to mind. ***'Please tell me you've at least spoken to Jack and Adi!'****.* *And who the fuck are Jack and... Hang on...* Unexpectedly, everything seemed to fall into place, like the missing piece of the puzzle had finally been found. ***'I ain't got a clue what the fuck you're playing at, but you said you wanted to talk, so talk.'****.* The silvery voice of the woman I had met in the kitchen yesterday came to mind, followed by the annoying guy opposite me. ***'Thinking about it, you also said you wanted to talk to me about something.'****. Are they Jack and Adi?...* I mulled, rubbing a hand across my jaw.

What am I meant to even be talking to them about? I had no idea, so I decided to find out.

"Anyway," I began, my eyes locking onto Jack's – *At least I presume he's Jack...* - before reshuffling the cards, "What was I meant to talk to you about yesterday or whenever it was?"

Shrugging, Jack retorted, "You tell me. You're the one who wanted to talk to me."

Not much help then...

Not giving up, I pressed, "So you haven't a clue what I wanted to talk to you and Adi about?"

I was a little confused by the momentary baffled glance Jack shot me. *What was all that about?* But it was gone before I could be sure.

"No, who do I look like? You?" He replied sharply, giving me a glassy stare, "Only **you** know what you wanted to talk to us about."

Fair point... But it still didn't sway from my ever-growing frustration.

"Right!" Jack suddenly exclaimed, clapping his hands once, "Are you going to show me poker? Or are you going to shuffle them all day?" His comment made me realise I was still shifting cards through the deck.

"Yeah, sure." I said, dealing myself two, "So now you need to check, bet or fol-"

"Mr Sadler," The venomous voice of Nurse Deadman sliced through the atmosphere, bringing with it an indescribable fear that engulfed not only me but notably Jack too.

I couldn't ignore how terrified he now looked. His face had turned ashen, tendons stood out on his neck, and his breaths were bursting in and out.

"It's time for your session with Doctor Sasin." Nurse Deadman continued, gaining my attention as her two puppy-dog orderlies appeared beside her.

Her stone-cold, blue eyes were fixated on Jack; her unpleasant, reptilian smile that I had grown accustomed to marred her unnaturally pretty face. *What does Doctor Sasin do to him?* I wondered, my eyes shifting back to Jack as he rose to his feet, discarding the cards on the table.

"You'll have to show me how to play poker some other time." He said with a forced grin, the two orderlies now firmly grasping him on either side.

He was then led away with Nurse Deadman taking the lead, and I watched until they disappeared into the corridor. *Now I know who Jack is; I just need to find Adi...* I thought as a baleful scream erupted in the room. I soon noted another squabble had started by the record player, but I ignored it and glanced over to the hallway where Jack had disappeared moments ago. *Hopefully, I'll get a chance to talk to him later.*

Rising to my feet, I searched for the woman I presumed was Adi. However, I soon realised mostly men occupied the asylum. *It'll be like trying to find a needle in a haystack...* I muttered, clocking a handful of women gathered by the bookshelf cackling like hens, but I didn't recognise them. Circling my attention to the record player, I spied some women launching themselves tooth and nail at the guy trying to change the music, but none were Adi. *Where is she?*

"THAT'S ENOUGH!" A nurse bellowed, trying to stop the fight, but was no match for all of them.

Whoa! I gasped when the inpatients turned on her, now ripping her hair and scratching at her face. *Isn't anyone gonna help?!* I glimpsed around, but the orderlies were too busy clearing the tables while nearby nurses just watched on, evidently not wanting to get involved.

Immediately feeling sorry for the nurse, I couldn't just stand by and watch her get beaten unfairly. *Why am I doing this?... Why?...*

Inhaling a steady breath, I advanced on the fight, hollering, "Hey! Leave her alone!"

I yanked the female patients off who were tearing into the nurse's flesh with their ragged nails; even the guy who tried changing the music was pummelling her with fists.

"**GET OFF!**" I roared, shoving everyone back so I was now between them.

To my relief, they were all distracted by the music again, so I pulled the nurse aside.

Grasping her by the tops of her arms, I asked, "Are you oka-"

CRACK!

Chapter Six

I should never have trusted him!

"Vell..." The German doctor called Kröger began in a bitter tone. He was perched on the edge of his desk in the middle of the white-walled, doctors' surgery-looking room. I had to squint a little to look at him as the barred window behind, overlooking the asylum grounds, flooded the room with sunshine. Not even the blinds did anything to alleviate the glaring light.

"Vat can I do fur you today?" He carried on, and I couldn't believe what he had said.

Is he serious?! I sat pinching the bridge of my broken nose to ease the bleeding while two orderlies stood on either side; the one on my left was so wide he almost touched the bed lengthways against the wall.

A forced smile grew on Doctor Kröger's lips when I didn't reply. He then crouched before me, his shiny black shoes scuffing the mottled brown carpet. I couldn't help but feel guilty when I took him in. A large bump was on his forehead, with butterfly stitches above his left eyebrow, showcasing his face in a motley of purples and reds. *I really did hurt him...* I murmured, lowering my gaze.

"So, how did you do zis?" Doctor Kröger pried, lowering my hand to inspect my nose.

Sighing, I recollected how one of the orderlies had punched me square in the face. I grimaced a little as the crunch of bone still echoed in my head when he practically smooshed it flat; not only was it sickening, but the pain that followed had me throw up.

I can't believe that nurse didn't stick up for me, vouch for what I did... Even those other nurses saw what happened and did nothing... I uttered, angered by the lack of justice I had received. *I honestly don't know why I expected any of them to help...* I thought the staff were still decent human beings somewhere deep down. *Again, I don't know why I assumed that...*

When I didn't reply, the orderly to my right spoke for me, "He was harassing Linda."

"I was **not** harassing her!" I corrected in a deep baritone, defending myself for what felt like the hundredth time, "I **saved** her from the patients attacking-"

"Shut it, you!" The other orderly snapped, backhanding me across the face and causing the throbbing pain in my nose to increase tenfold.

"Nein, nein, it's quite all right!" Doctor Kröger assured, raising his hand.

His blue eyes circled back to me, and he said, "Nobody likes a liar."

"I'm **not** a liar!" I declared through gritted teeth, but my words may as well have fallen on deaf ears as he merely began inspecting my nose once more.

He doesn't believe me... I muttered, frustrated. *No one believes me...*

"I should've just left her and gone to find whoever Adi is..." I uttered under my breath.

"Adi?" Doctor Kröger echoed, pulling back to look at me in confusion, "Zee shtrange, curly-haired boy? But you schare a room viz him..."

Wait, what?! Shocked, I couldn't stop my jaw from dropping. *So he's Adi, not Jack?* A sudden coldness expanded in my core. *Then who the hell is Jack?!*

"Anyway," Doctor Kröger piped up, sitting back on his heels, "Just as I sought. Broken."

He reached for a mirror on his desk, showing me my reflection while saying, "See. Broken."

How stupid does he think I am?! I fumed as he stood up, advancing on the waist-high white cabinet along the right-hand wall. *I **know** it's broken! I can **feel** it!*

"It needs to be put back in place." Doctor Kröger explained, rummaging in the top drawer and producing

something that resembled gauze, "Vich is a schame."
It took a moment for his comment to sink in, but when it did, I wondered, "What's a shame?"

"You look better viz a broken nose." He clarified, "Suits your face."

Wait, what?! I gaped, shocked, as he wandered back over, gesturing to the orderlies with a nod. *Did he really just say that?!*

Doctor Kröger then rolled up the sleeves of his white coat before crouching back down in front of me, saying, "Just a snap."

The orderlies then grasped me by the tops of my arms, firmly holding me in place as I blurted, "Wait!" But Doctor Kröger ignored me and lunged for my face, sharply yanking my nose with an ear-crunching crack; an excruciating howl erupted out of me.

***

Ughhh... My head... I groaned, resisting the urge to pinch the bridge of my nose to alleviate the agonising headache. Pressing a hand to my forehead, I tried to ignore the incessant noise from the movie playing at full volume in the busy recreation room. It was projected on the wall where the TV once was. The orderlies had set all the chairs up in rows facing the movie; I was sat furthest away by the bookshelf, using one of the chairs in front as a footstall.

'We're running out of time.' Doctor Hailey's voice reverberated in the back of my mind, fuelling the excruciating headache. *I really don't wanna think about this right now...* But my stubborn thoughts refused to let up. *Why does he want me to talk to Jack and Adi? And what's with all the evidence?* So many questions bombarded me, but his suspicious behaviour had me wondering if he had an ulterior motive. *He clearly needs me for something. But if I do his bidding, will he just throw me under the bus afterwards?* I had no reason to trust this man. *Nor any reason not to...* A voice quietly added.

Sighing, the curiosity within grew and grew until it became almost unbearable. *Fuck it! I need to know what's going on!* Hastily rising to my feet, I peered around, spotting two nurses lingering beside the door that led to the kitchen.

"Hi, yeah, excuse me." I began as I drew near, and the annoyance plastered upon their faces made me believe I had interrupted their conversation.
"Can you show me where Jack is?" I asked, and one bluntly ordered, "Sit back down!"
"Even if you just point him out or tell me where he is." I persisted, only for the other to threaten, "Right, if you don't sit back down now, I'll get one of the orderlies to take you to Doctor Sasin!"
I immediately shut up, terrified of the consequences. *No, I can't see him!* My heart beat so hard it started to give me chest pains. *I can't have him put me through all that again!* Just the thought of Metrazol therapy had me trembling.
"Okay, sorry!" I swiftly apologised, waving my hands in a no gesture, "I'll just head back to my seat."
I then skulked away before they could change their minds. Once I sat down, I buried my face in my hands, muttering under my breath, "What the fuck do I do?... I'm running out of time..."
"Perhaps I can be of assistance, brother." A voice, sounding like the groaning of a gallows, chilled me to my very core.
I lowered my hands, peering to my right and seeing a scrawny-looking man sitting beside me. *And how exactly can he help?* I mulled, staring into his cunning blue eyes that bulged forebodingly from his gaunt face wreathed in smiles, showing off his rotten and cracked teeth. A fine layer of light brown stubble graced his jawline, matching his swept-back, receding hair.
Sitting straight, I curiously wondered, "And how can **you** help me? You don't even know what I need help with."
Gesturing to the nurses with a nod, he replied, "I overheard." He paused momentarily, as if to let that sink in, before continuing, "I can get ya ter Jack."
"Really?!" I blurted, shocked, "How?"
His sly smirk pulled at the corner of his thin, unkind lips as he said, "Trust me, it's best ya don't know. Just... Go with the flow... The motion of things... Ya get?" And I instantly didn't trust him.
There was something about this patient that I couldn't quite put my finger on. He reminded me of one of those Italian-American guys who strived to be part of the mafia. *Thinking about it, he looks like that guy from Reservoir Dogs.* I couldn't think of the actor's name but vividly remembered who he

played. He was the one who hated the name he was assigned: Mr Pink. *But I don't have much choice. Otherwise, how else am I gonna find Jack?*

"Alright," I reluctantly began, "Then what do we-"

"Ah-ah-ah!" He interrupted with a wag of his index finger, "If I do this for ya, then ya owe me a favour." A bloodcurdling grin manifested on his face, "**Any** favour."

Any?! I repeated with a shake of my head. *I'm not that stupid!*

"If you expect me to kill someone, then you can just forget it!"

He was momentarily silent, clearly mulling it over. *So he did want me to kill someone...* I presumed, shivering at that notion.

"Fine, fine, fine." He disappointedly agreed, "I won't ask ya ter kill anyone." He then did the two-finger salute, "Scouts 'onour."

Yet I still didn't trust him.

Pushing the desire to get as far away from him as possible, I reminded myself I **had** to find Jack.

"Okay," I began, cutting straight to the point, "So what do we-"

"Randall." He interrupted, grasping my hand and giving it a firm, almost intimidating shake, "But everyone calls me Randy, if ya get what I mean."

He nudged me in the ribs with his elbow, giving me a wink as he chuckled. *O... Kay...*

Forcing an awkward laugh, I apprehensively pulled my hand free, replying, "Travis."

"Well, Travis," Randy started, "Mind if I call ya Trav?"

I didn't get the chance to respond before he went off on a tangent, "The plan begins in the lavboratory."

Lav-bor-atory?... I repeated, slightly confused. *Does he mean lavatory?*

"I'll go first, make sure the balls rollin', plans in motion, then ya give it a few moments before comin' with. Ya get?"

Why do we need to go to the toilets?

Keeping my thoughts to myself, I nodded, "Yeah, I get."

Without warning, Randy rose to his feet, leaving me staring after him in horror. *Wait, does he mean **now**?!* I panicked when he advanced on the nurses. *I didn't think he meant right now!*

"Ladies!" I heard him proclaim over the movie in a sickly-sweet timbre, "I'm in dire need of a piss, so why don't ya get an orderly over 'ere ter take me ter the John real quick!"

Unfazed by his behaviour, one of the nurses beckoned over an orderly who guided him out of the recreation room.

As I circled my attention downcast, I couldn't help but worry. *Was this a mistake? Getting involved with someone like him?* Something about him made my throat feel constricted, something slimy and conniving that had my mind going to worst-case scenarios. *What if he stabs me or something in the toilet?* But I knew I couldn't back out now in fear of upsetting him. *And then who knows what he'd do to me...*

With a shake of my head, I begrudgingly wandered back over to the nurses, who looked far from impressed when they noticed me.

"What now?" The one who told me to sit down first grumbled. *I hope I'm doing the right thing...* I prayed, but a little apprehensive voice piped up. *What if I'm not? What if all this goes wrong, and I end up dead? My kids will be without a father...* Then my mind began to create a mental tally of other unbearable outcomes.

"Well?" The nurse urged after a moment of silence.

I knew I needed to make a decision now. *I either back out and leave that guy high and dry, or I just go with it and hope for the best...*

Gripping my hands together, I wetted my lips and answered, "I... I need to use the toilet."

A sigh of frustration seeped from her lips, as if it were a massive inconvenience.

Shifting her attention away from me, the nurse waved her hand and yelled, "JAY!"

I followed her line of sight to see the orderly, who I had dubbed Statham, strut towards us.

When he was a stone's throw away, he wondered, "Is he causing you trouble?"

"Nah," She shook her head, "He just needs the loo."

Nodding, Statham firmly grabbed me by the arm, towing me out of the recreation room and into the hallway. He soon pulled me to a halt by a door along the left-hand wall, which I recognised as the one Doctor Hailey had pinned me beside. *This is it.* I fretted as Statham opened it. *No going back.* He then went to take a step inside but stopped mid-step, holding the door ajar. From where I stood, I could see the off-white tiled walls from floor to ceiling.

"Ray, I didn't know you were in here." Statham commented, to which the man inside replied, "Just watching this guy."

I presumed he was the orderly who had escorted Randy.

"But if you want to wait outside," Ray continued, "Just take my guy back when he's done, and I'll watch yours."

"Sounds like a plan!" Statham nodded before circling his attention down to me, growling, "Get inside, now!"

I didn't get the chance to react before he snatched me up by the front of my shirt, pulling me close and tossing me inside the stupidly small room.

"Hurry up and piss." The orderly inside, who looked scarily similar to Steve Austin, implored, gaining my attention.

Seriously, what's with all the orderlies looking like they've stepped off the set of Rambo?!

Austin – *I mean Ray!* - was leaning against the furthest metal sink along the left-hand wall. Matching toilets were mirrored on the right, with no walls or curtains in between to offer privacy. That was when I clocked Randy using the toilet with his back to the ever-watchful orderly.

BANG! The door then slammed shut, distracting me for a split second, but it was long enough for Randy to turn to the sinks.

"**HEY, TRAV!**" He exclaimed obnoxiously loud, seemingly surprised to see me.

Why's he acting so shocked? I wondered, but that thought was swiftly forgotten when he unexpectedly grabbed Ray by the throat with mind-blowingly quick reflexes.

"**FANCY SEEIN' YA IN 'ERE!**" He continued blissfully, smashing the orderly's face against the wall with bone-shattering ferocity.

It was at that exact moment I knew I had made a massive mistake trusting him.

"What the fuck have you done?!" I panicked when Randy released the orderly, who collapsed to the floor with an almighty thud.

I should never have trusted him! Blood cascaded down Ray's face; a cracked and gory wall tile was left in his wake. *I should* ***never*** *have fucking trusted him!* But it wasn't the orderly who I was concerned about; I was terrified for my own life.

"Shut yer mouth and relax! 'e ain't dead!" Randy urged in a hushed tone.

I immediately shut my mouth, fearful of upsetting him. *I need to calm down!* I exhaled, shooting the unconscious orderly a quick glance, certain I couldn't see him breathing. *Fuck! He's dead! He's fucking dead!* A sudden and overwhelming sense of dread then encompassed me. *What the fuck are we gonna do?! It'll only be a matter of time until someone finds-*

"This is just part of the plan." Randy interrupted my frightened thoughts.

Plan?! I gaped, my head snapping over to him.

"**It is?!**" I bawled, but he shushed me again with a frantic wave of his hand.

"I said ter shut yer fuckin' mouth!" He barked through bared teeth, "Unless ya want someone ter 'ear us!"

It was then I remembered the orderly waiting outside. *Shit!* My heart was now beating so fast that it made my chest tingle. *What's gonna happen when he comes in and sees **this**?!*

"Put 'is uniform on." Randy ordered, dragging me back to the conversation, "Make sure yer got 'is keys. I'll meet ya back in the rec room, ya get?"

"Wait, what?!" I gawked, trying to process everything he had just said.

Why the hell do I need to wear his uniform?! I had no idea what Randy had planned, but I would do anything to turn back time and decline his offer. *Then none of this would be fucking happening!*

"Then what?!" I hastily inquired, sweeping my hand toward the motionless orderly, "And what about him?! What about the one outside?!"

"Just shut up!" Randy snapped angrily, pounding his fist against the wall and making me recoil.

I thought I saw something shift in his unnerving blue eyes, like a ticking time bomb waiting to explode, but it was gone before I could be sure.

"Keep yer voice down!" He added in a quiet undertone, nodding towards the door, "'e'll take me back, thinkin' 'e's-" He abruptly kicked the unconscious orderly in the gut, "Watchin' ya."

"Wait-" I began when he turned to leave, "What am I-"

"Tell the nurses yer'll take me ter my room ter calm down when ya come back." He swiftly intervened.

"Calm down?" I repeated, confused, "Why do you need to calm-" But he left before I could finish, leaving me worrying about what he had planned.

My eyes then drifted back down to Ray, locking onto his bloodstained white shirt. *Shit!* I cursed, bringing both hands up to grasp the sides of my head when trepidation set in. *What the fuck am I gonna do?! You'd have to be as thick as two fucking planks not to notice!* Then an idea came to mind, allowing the doubt within to dwindle. *I could just walk away, forget all this happened and pretend I wasn't part of it.* But I knew I would never escape Randy whilst I was still in the asylum, and a cold sweat instantly consumed me. *He'll kill me if I don't go through with this!* Just that thought alone caused the hairs on the nape of my neck to rise.

Reluctantly, I took off my clothes and pulled on the orderly's uniform. The blood-soaked shirt clung to my torso, making me grimace. *I can't believe I'm doing this...* Hoisting up the trousers, I heard the jangle of metal, so I checked the pockets and found the keys Randy had requested. *I really can't believe I'm doing this...* I uttered whilst staring down at Ray's bare body, his white briefs the only thing preserving his dignity.

Once I scooped up my clothes and hid them behind one of the toilets, I hesitantly stepped out into the corridor, half expecting to see Statham still waiting. *Wait, where is everyone?* To my surprise, the entire hallway was dead, so quiet I would have heard a pin drop. *Why's it so quiet?* But that deliberation was short-lived when a ruckus suddenly resounded from the recreation room, and Randy instantly came to mind. *What's he doing?* I approached apprehensively, dreading what I would be walking into.

However, I soon realised something. *What am I doing? There's no one around! I could just leave!* That notion halted me in my tracks. *I could walk right out of here.* Casting a glance around, there was still no one in sight, and that was when I made an immediate dash for the reception. *I can't believe I'm finally getting outta this hellhole!* I giddily proclaimed. *Fuck that crazy patient! Fuck Doctor Hailey and whoever the hell Jack is! Fuck the lot-* But I came to a sliding halt when I was a stone's throw from the end of the hallway, recognising the cold-blooded face of Nurse Deadman when she rounded the corner.

FUCK! I panicked when she approached with her two puppy-dog orderlies, so I swiftly about-turned, hoping they didn't notice me. *Shit, shit, shit! What am I gonna do?!* But deep down, I knew, and my eyes anxiously locked onto the recreation room entrance as I sped towards it. *I hope they don't come in here- Oh for fuck's sake...* My unease vanished, replaced with disbelief when I saw Randy throw chairs at whoever came within a three-inch radius of him. *What the hell is he doing-* Then the clip-clop of heels distracted me. *Fuck this!* I exclaimed in frustration when Nurse Deadman wandered in with her two henchmen. *Fuck this entire situation!*

Knowing she would recognise me dressed in orderly garb, I hurried over to the commotion. Randy's unnerving blue eyes locked onto me as I drew nearer, a silent communication for me to step in. *If it weren't for Nurse Deadman, I could've been out of here by now...* Instead, I was playing a dangerous game where anyone could recognise me at any given moment. *I need to get out of here before someone does.*

"Leave him with me." I heedlessly informed the nurse and orderlies trying to deal with Randy, "I'll take him back to his room to calm down."

"I'm begging your pardon, but **I** was the one giving orders, not you!" The nurse barked, aghast, and my stomach instantly dropped with consternation as I didn't want to cause a scene. Then I noticed the two orderlies; they blatantly stared me up and down before exchanging bewildered glances. *Do they know I'm not one of them?!* Then I spotted Nurse Deadman out of the corner of my eye, quietly observing the situation. *Shit!*

"Who are y-" One of the orderlies began; however, the nurse swiftly interrupted, "Why's there blood on you?"

What? Following her line of sight, I stared down in horror at my bloodstained white shirt. *Fuck!* I had completely forgotten about it in my haste to leave. *What do I say?!*

Frantically staring between the nurse and orderlies, I knew I needed to act fast, so I blurted, "He punched me!" And I gestured between Randy and my broken nose.

"Aaaaah!" She nodded in understanding, "You want to return the favour, I see."

"Yes, yes!" I hastily agreed, anxiously aware the two orderlies were still glaring sceptically at me.

*They **know** I'm not one of them!*

"Fine, but don't **ever** undermine me again." The nurse warned, flicking her hand for me to go and deal with Randy. Nodding once, I sped over before either of the two orderlies could say anything. *I just hope this other guy doesn't realise I'm not one of them as well.*

"Leave him with me; I've got this." I said to the orderly, who was trying to grab the chair Randy was thrusting at him.

"Be my guest." He scoffed, stepping back.

The tension visibly oozed from Randy's body, and I knew now was my chance. Grabbing the legs, I ripped the chair from his grasp, causing him to stagger into my hold.

"How the fuck did you do that?!" The orderly gasped as I adjusted my grip, holding Randy by the back of his shirt.

Shrugging, I replied blasé, "Just better than you, I guess."

I didn't wait for a response before pushing Randy toward the exit, using him as a shield to hide from onlookers.

"About time ya showed up..." Randy quietly uttered when we stepped out into the corridor, "Ya 'ad me thinkin' ya did a runner for a sec."

Part of me wondered whether he somehow knew of my attempt to escape. *Don't be stupid! How would he know?*

Pulling him aside, I asked in a hushed tone, "Where are we going?"

"Female ward." He replied matter-of-factly, and I couldn't help but shoot him a bewildered glance.

Female ward? I repeated. *Why are we going there?* But I kept my thoughts to myself, fearful he wouldn't react well to me questioning him.

"And where exactly is the female ward?" I wondered, and Randy queried in disbelief, "Ya don't know where the female ward is?"

Should I? I worried, unable to ignore the surprise shimmering behind his unnerving blue eyes.

He then gestured towards the reception, "Just turn left at the end of the corridor."

Nodding, I pushed him onwards, still using him as a shield.

Why should I know where the female ward is? I fretted, practically hearing the cogs turn in his head, knowing he knew something didn't add up. *I'm a guy for crying out loud! I don't need to know!*

Trying not to dwell on my troubled thoughts, I cast my gaze to the reception once we turned left out of the corridor. *This would've been a perfect time to escape!* I moaned in despair as it was empty; even the surrounding area was eerily quiet. *Where is everyone?*

We then passed a grand-looking, oak double door on our right, which didn't fit in with the rest of the décor throughout the asylum. A brass cross was in the middle, divided by both doors. *Is that a church?*

"'ow long 'ave ya been admitted 'ere?" Randy abruptly asked, distracting me.

That was when I noticed we passed the hallway leading to the infirmary on our left. Even now, I could vividly hear Doctor Kröger snap my nose back into place, making me shudder.

"Cat got yer tongue?" Randy mocked when I didn't reply.

What's with all the questions?! He clearly knew there was more to me than I was letting on, but he was the last person I would trust with my predicament.

"I swear, I've seen ya for a few months now." He said as we passed the barred windows on either side of the wide corridor.

The afternoon sun poured in, momentarily blinding me.

"Long enough..." I murmured, glancing at the gravel track leading to the gate out of this hellhole to our right, "I've been here long enough..."

If it weren't for Nurse Deadman, I could've been outta here by now... A dejected sigh leaked from my lips.

"'aven't we all?" Randy chuckled, nudging me in the ribs.

Forcing a laugh, I couldn't hold his gaze a moment longer and focused on the courtyard out the window to our left.

We then reached the end, and the only way to go was left, leading to a gated entrance.

"**This** is the female ward." Randy explained as I peered through the bars, spotting metal doors on either side.

It looked identical to the hallway I had been dragged up and down on the other side of the asylum. *So that must mean that's the male ward.* I presumed, my mental map now expanding as I got a clearer image of the building layout.

"Oit!" Randy growled, gaining my attention, "Ya gonna just stand there all day, or are ya gonna fuckin' open it?!"

Retrieving the keys from my trouser pocket, I fiddled with them

for a few minutes, searching for the right one.
"Any day now..." He uttered.
I don't know which one opens it! It took every ounce of self-control to stop myself from snapping; instead, I focused on the task until I finally unlocked the gate.

I barely even opened it before Randy barged inside, making me stagger backwards with an oof. *Fuck you then!* I bristled, having to grind my teeth as a deterrent from erupting like a volcano. I watched with cold, flinty eyes as Randy quickly but quietly hurried down the cream-walled corridor, his shoes barely rapping against the dark, hardwood floor. *And off he fucks...*

Inhaling a deep, calming breath, I expelled it in one big puff before stepping inside, freezing when I heard murmurs echo behind some of the doors. *It sounds like they're in pain...* I deliberated just before Randy reappeared.
"No one else is 'ere." He triumphantly grinned, and my body unexpectedly released all the built-up tension I didn't know I was harbouring.
Hopefully, it stays that way.

"But we better 'urry." He added, moving toward the closest door on the left, "We shouldn't be 'ere." Just those words alone reminded me we didn't have much time.
I still need to change back into my clothes before someone finds that orderly! But I doubted I would be so lucky. *I don't know how I'm gonna get away with thi-*
"Oit!" Randy barked, dragging me out of my fretful thoughts, "Check the right side!" He shuttered the peephole with a clang before dashing to the next door.

"How do you even know Jack's here?" I questioned, checking the first door.
I could hardly see inside the dimly lit cell when I opened the peephole. What I thought were mattresses were pressed lengthwise along the left and right concrete walls. Something resembling a toilet was in the far right-hand corner above the bed. *I can't see anyone in here...*

Moving to the next door, I carried on before Randy could reply to my previous question, "And who is Jack?"
Freezing mid-step, Randy's bulbous eyes protruded more than humanly possible when he gaped at me, "'**Who is Jack?**'?!"

Shouldn't I have asked that?... I wondered in uncertainty, feeling my breath catch in my chest as he stared at me.

After a moment of silence, Randy regained himself and commented, "Look, I ain't a clue what the doctors are doin' to ya, but yer got a screw loose or somethin'. Ya get?"

No, I don't get! I inwardly fumed, momentarily clenching my hands into fists.

He must have noted my frustration as he quickly added, "I just guessed ya knew 'er... Why else would ya want ter talk ter 'er?..." That comment brought me up short.

'Her'?! I knew it should have been obvious – *Seeing as we're in the female ward* – but having it confirmed was still a massive surprise. *Was she the one in the kitchen?*

"Look, we ain't got much time!" Randy stated, checking the doors once more, "Just keep a watch or somethin' while I find 'er."

He's right! I panicked. *It'll only be a matter of time before someone finds that orderly or us!* Glancing back at the gated entrance, I kept watch while Randy searched for Jack. *But what if she's not here? What then?*

I had no idea how long I had been waiting, but it felt like a lifetime before Randy beckoned me down with a wave of his hand.

"Trav, I found 'er!" He hollered, making me cringe in fear that someone had heard him.

Is he trying to get us caught?! When I heard no footsteps, I rushed down the corridor only to realise Randy stood a stone's throw from a gated entrance along the left. *Shit! Is that solitary confinement?!* I wasn't brave enough to see if a guard was stationed. *I just hope they've not heard us!*

Randy then moved away from the cell door, so I gazed inside and saw a blonde girl lying on a mattress. At first, I didn't recognise her. *Who was that girl in the kitchen then?* But when she rolled over, I spotted the shaved head. *It **is** her!* I gasped in relief, stumbling back a step before fumbling with the keys.

"Just 'urry up!" Randy growled after I tried several keys; it was just my luck that the last one worked.

Leaving it in the lock, I hurried inside, my shoes thudding against the concrete floor. I then turned to slam the door behind me; however, Randy unexpectedly followed.

"What the fuck you doing?!" I loudly exclaimed.

He didn't get the chance to respond as a silvery voice piped up, "Ricky?"

My eyes snapped over to Jack, who was now propped up on her elbows.

"Who the fuck's Ricky?" Randy confusedly asked.

I didn't have the time to explain, so I snapped, "Just get out! **NOW!**"

"I wouldn't be so hasty, Trav." He wickedly retorted, a one-sided smirk growing on his callous face, "Ya owe me a favour, remember?"

Seriously?! I gawked, shocked. *He wants **this** as his favour?!*

"What the hell's going on?!" Jack interjected, staring between us sceptically, "And who's Trav?"

I don't have the fucking time to explain all of this!

"Look, I don't have much time!" I heatedly proclaimed, my eyes narrowing at Randy, "So you just stay there for all I care, but keep your mouth shut!"

I then glanced back down at Jack, "Apparently, I need to talk to you."

I just hope she knows something.

Swinging her legs around to sit on the edge of the mattress, Jack blatantly stared me up and down. *What's she looking at?*

She then gestured at me with a nod, "Who did you kill?"

What? I couldn't help but furrow my brow before following her gaze to my bloodstained clothes, a coldness expanding within my core. *Shit!*

"I didn't kill anyone!" I desperately hawked, my attention snapping back to her.

At least, I hope not. A little voice echoed in the back of my mind.

Sighing, Jack rose to her feet, "I can see you're not in the mood..." She commented with an irritated shake of her head.

"In the mood?" I repeated, baffled, "In the mood for what?"

Confusion then contorted her face, which only added to mine.

What the hell's going on?

"What's wrong with you, Ricky?" She questioned after a thoughtful moment of silence, "You're not normally this serious. Or miserable..."

"I'm **not** miserable!" I bit back, but then I realised we were going off-topic, "Anyway, this isn't why I'm here!"

Before I could continue, Jack defensively retorted, "And if this is what I think it's about, I've **repeatedly** told you I'll come and find you when I've made up my mind!"

Made up her mind?! I echoed despairingly. *Made up her mind about what?!* I now found myself with more questions than I had answers.

Jack must have sensed my frustration as her features softened, and she sympathetically said, "I know you and Hailey are running out of time, but what you're asking for is a lot!"

"Up ter somethin' with Doctor Hailey, hmm?..." Randy piped up, gaining my attention; his eyes had lit up like a kid on Christmas morning.

Right then, I knew I should have kicked him out before speaking to Jack. *I need to end this conversation now before he knows too much!*

Gazing back at Jack, I had no idea what I had asked of her, but I hastily acknowledged her comment, "Yes, yes, I know I'm asking for a lot, but I just need to know-"

"It's not as simple as that, and you **promised** me you understood!" She angrily interrupted, grief and shame glistening behind her sky-blue eyes.

"If I wear that camera, I'll be admitting **everything** he does to me!" She said, disgusted and embarrassed, "I won't be able to ignore it any more like I have been. It'll no longer be a nightmare but a reality."

Wait, what? Who's she talking about? And what did they do to her?

Suddenly, the clip-clop of heels echoed in the corridor, chilling me to my core. *Fuck!* I panicked; even Jack and Randy looked equally on edge with wide, anxious eyes. *Please don't come in! Please don't come in!*

I then heard a woman's voice that I didn't recognise, "Make sure Miranda's put in another cell tonight. We can't risk her smothering Brandy after her sess..." But she unexpectedly trailed off, leaving me waiting with bated breath.

What's going on?

The clip of the woman's heels rushed toward Jack's cell. Then, abruptly, she gawked in disbelief, "Who on earth left their keys in the door?!" Her words were like a punch to the gut, knocking the wind right out of me.

Hurriedly searching my pockets, a sudden and overwhelming

sense of dread encompassed me when I couldn't find the keys. *Shit!*

The metal door then opened with a shriek as it scraped against the concrete floor. Light bathed our faces as a horrified gasp sliced through the atmosphere.

"What on earth are you two doing in here?!" The nurse demanded before two imposing orderlies appeared on either side of her.

I could feel the blood drain from my face when they blatantly stared me up and down, clocking the uniform. *I'm gonna be in deep fucking shit...*

***

"Richard, Richard, Richard..." Doctor Sasin murmured as he paced behind his desk, pinching the bridge of his nose as if he had a lingering headache.

"Why are you causing me so many problems?" He wondered, lowering his hand and staring at me with his glacial blue eyes, which instilled me with an indescribable fear.

What's he gonna do with me?! I fretted, wanting to escape the gas chamber chair I was strapped to, but I didn't dare budge an inch. Instead, I averted my attention downcast as his impenetrable gaze became too much. Then I saw Nurse Deadman come to stand on my left, aware her two puppy-dog orderlies were on either side of me but just out of sight.

"One member of staff has been concussed **twice** because of you!" Doctor Sasin declared heatedly, gaining my attention, "And another has been transferred to a nearby hospital!"

"But I didn't do anything to that order-" I tried to defend myself, but he swiftly interrupted my testimony, "I have had enough of your lies, Mr Moon!" Then his glacial blue eyes shifted to Nurse Deadman, "Take him straight to solitary confinement."

Undeterred, I vowed, "But I've done nothing wr-"

"Then why are you wearing a member of staff's uniform if you did nothing?" Doctor Sasin intervened again, gesturing to the bloody garb with a sweep of his hand.

I didn't know what to say that would convince him of my innocence, so I circled my eyes downcast and kept my mouth shut. *None of this would be happening if I hadn't listened to Randy!*

"Make sure you pick up a change of clothes for Mr Moon." Doctor Sasin instructed, distracting me from my ponderings.

"Of course, Doctor." Nurse Deadman replied, unfastening the straps around my arms.

It was at that moment I wondered if I could make a run for it. *Don't be so stupid!* A voice in the back of my mind scolded. *How are you gonna get past the locked gates?*

All hope of escape swiftly vanished as the orderlies hoisted me to my feet, dragging me out into the corridor and following Nurse Deadman. I wanted to talk to her, to tell her my side of the story, but I knew there was no point as my words would only fall on deaf ears. *And even if she did believe me, she's quite clearly loyal to Doctor Sasin...* So I kept my mouth shut and my head down.

Once Nurse Deadman had picked up a clean pair of clothes, we headed straight to solitary confinement via the side route.

"Morning, Cora." The stationed guard cheerfully greeted her.

Ignoring him, she bluntly asked, "What room is available?"

Retrieving the clipboard from the wooden table, he glanced at it momentarily before replying, "Number nineteen."

"Leave it blank." She instructed, and he nodded before discarding the clipboard.

The guard then granted us access, and the orderlies dragged me left down the corridor to the end, coming to a halt by the last door on the right. As soon as Nurse Deadman unlocked it, she gestured with a sharp wave of her hand for the orderlies to throw me inside. I staggered into the concrete bed, my shins hitting it with a crack. Suppressing the urge to cry out in pain, I hunched over, breathing through the suffering throbbing full force in my legs. *Just breathe... Just breat-*

"Do whatever you wish with him." Nurse Deadman's venomous voice sliced through my thoughts.

Wait, what?! My head snapped over to her just as I opened my mouth to speak, but I couldn't find the words I wanted to say as I was too horrified. *She... She doesn't mean that, does she?...* I fretted as she tossed the clothes onto the bed before the two orderlies loomed in the doorway, causing an uncontrollable shudder to sweep throughout my body.

"I'll be just outside." Nurse Deadman added with her infamous reptilian smile, making my chest tighten as fear crept in.

No, no, no! I panicked when the orderlies stepped inside, and she closed the metal door, plunging us into darkness. *They can't do this! It's illegal!* I backed away until I was pressed against the wall between the bed and the toilet, hoping to remain hidden. Then the peephole opened with a rattle, illuminating the room, and I was instantly consumed with dread.

A bloodcurdling grin grew on Stallone's face when his eyes landed on me, and an otherworldly growl seeped from his lips as he said, "Let's see how well you fare."

Pressing myself harder against the cold, tiled wall, I tremulously wondered, "Wuh-Wuh-What are you guh-going to do to muh-me?"

"You'll see." He replied while cracking his knuckles.

It all happened so fast that I didn't even have time to react. Stallone lunged for the front of my bloody shirt, yanking me towards him, and I was met with a ruthless fist. It would have sent me tumbling backwards if it weren't for his impenetrable hold. A groan escaped me as a gush of hot blood pissed out of my nose, hitting the floor with a pitter-patter.

When Stallone tugged me back towards him, Schwarzenegger's fist was ready for the next blow, so powerful Stallone lost his grip, and I collided into the wall with an almighty thud. I could have sworn I spat out a handful of teeth as I slid down onto my arse, but I was immediately hoisted back onto my feet by the scruff of my hair.

CRUNCH! My face was slammed into the wall, my nose flattening to one side before something wet and sticky streamed down my mouth.

Spitting out the copper liquid lingering on my tongue, I desperately pleaded, "**STOP!**" But whoever had a hold on me propelled me back towards the wall.

SMASH! Blood pooled in my mouth when I accidentally sunk my teeth into my tongue. **CRACK!** A couple more teeth shattered on impact, bubbling out my mouth along with more hot gore.

Lights danced in my eyes when I was finally pulled back, but I was too dazed to do anything. I didn't even have the strength to fight when my clothes were torn from me, physically yanking me with the motion.

Just when I thought the orderlies had finished with me as I crumbled to the floor, one of them – I couldn't tell who – yanked me back up by my hair.

"This is for Ray!" He avenged before slamming my face into the cold, metal toilet with such force I was rendered into darkness.

Chapter Seven

Yer'll fuckin' regret makin' an enemy outta me!

I had no idea how long I had been in solitary confinement, and during that time, Stallone and Schwarzenegger had paid me more visits than my body could handle. Not only that, but my brain also felt fried after two sessions of Metrazol therapy and one electroconvulsive therapy, so I couldn't think straight even if I wanted to.

The only thing I could register as I lay motionless on the concrete bed facing the tiled wall was pain. The lingering darkness eased my persistent headache, but I couldn't tolerate the merciless pounding in my face as well as the insufferable body aches. I would have crawled out of my skin if it were physically possible.

Voices then steadily overpowered the headache, giving me something else to focus on. At first, it was just an assortment of pitches, but as they drew nearer, I could vaguely make out an articulate, masculine tone.

CLONK! A key unexpectedly turned in the lock, causing my heart to race so fast it gave me chest pains. It felt like only moments ago I was dragged to the therapy room; surely it wasn't time for another session. The door then opened with a shriek, and light now bathed the cell. I swiftly closed my eyes as the brightness felt like a thousand shards of glass stabbing into my brain.

"Just put him in-" The articulate voice cut himself off; I thought I recognised it but didn't have the mental strength to pinpoint who.

After a moment of silence, he snapped, "What's this patient doing in here?! He **wasn't** on the list!"

A long pause ensued; I thought he had left, but then he said in a slightly calmer tone, "Go and check what rooms are available while I deal with this."

The rap of shoes then echoed in my cell, causing fear to grip me like a vice; I couldn't face another session so soon. He then tried to roll me over onto my back, but I fought with what little strength I had left until I physically couldn't. When he pinned me down, I wanted nothing more than to run and hide, the sense of impending doom encompassing me so much that I started to hyperventilate.

I expected at any moment to be hoisted to my feet and dragged away; instead, he released his hold on me and questioned in disbelief, "Rick?!"

Slowly, I blinked one eye open to see Doctor Hailey peering down at me in concern. All fear seeped out of my body, replaced with relief as I emitted a huge breath. I wanted nothing more than to embrace him tightly and profusely thank him for being here, but I just didn't have the energy to talk, never mind keep my eye open for a moment longer.

"**I NEED SOMEONE IN HERE NOW!**" Doctor Hailey abruptly bellowed before a rush of footsteps infiltrated the cell, my eyes snapping open in fear the orderlies had returned to give me another beating.

"I need you two to take him straight to the infirmary!" Doctor Hailey instructed two orderlies whom I didn't recognise.

I immediately relaxed and closed my eyes, knowing I was actually safe.

Big hands then grasped me by the tops of my arms, hoisting me to my feet. I merely slumped in their holds despite trying with all my might to stand, my head flopping forward as if it had been snapped. The squeak of my shoes being dragged along the floor then resounded down the hallway as we made our way, I presumed, to the gated entrance, the clunk of metal confirming my suspicions.

"I'll be along shortly." Doctor Hailey commented.

I was then lugged away to the left while he began interrogating someone, "Firstly, why was that patient in here when his name isn't on the list?!" His heated voice gradually faded as the clip-clop of heels invaded the atmosphere.

"And secondly, who put him-"

"What do you think you're doing with Doctor Sasin's patient?!" A venomous voice sharply interrupted him; I didn't need to open my eyes to know it was Nurse Deadman.

Unfortunately, as their voices dwindled in the distance, I didn't hear what else was said. Aside from the usual commotion throughout the asylum, nothing else piqued my interest as the orderlies continued to heave me to the infirmary.

I couldn't comprehend how much time had passed before I was picked up bridal-style and plonked down on a surprisingly comfortable bed. Then again, I was certain anything would feel comfortable after that horrendous concrete one. *Are... Are we here?...* It was the first thought I had been able to muster, but I still didn't have the energy to do anything else.

"Should we strap him down?" One orderly queried, and I couldn't help but worry I had been taken to a treatment room. Opening my eyes, I swiftly shut them again with a hiss of pain. The light that seeped in through the window along the back wall increased my throbbing headache tenfold.

"Nah, look at him." The other responded, "He ain't gonna do shit!"

I would have loved to have proven him wrong, but he was right; I couldn't even keep my eyes open, never mind try to escape.

"Serves him right after what he did to Ray." The first orderly commented, making me bristle.

I did ***nothing*** *to him!* I adamantly declared, grinding my teeth, but it soon became unbearable due to the pain lingering in my jaw.

"I'm surprised Tim and Tom didn't kill him." The second chuckled, "Because I would've."

The anger bubbling within gave me the strength to finally open my eyes, noting I was in the doctor's surgery-looking room.

Through gritted teeth, I growled, "I didn't-" But the door opened with a squeak, and in stepped Doctor Hailey, who fixed his dark eyes on the orderlies.

"I need you both to leave." He commanded, and the second orderly questioned, "What? Even after what he did to Ray? You don't want us here?"

"Yes, even after what he did to Ray." Doctor Hailey retorted in frustration, "Now leave!"

The orderlies shot one another concerned glances but didn't say anything and left.

As soon as the door slammed shut, Doctor Hailey rounded on me and gutturally roared, "What's this I hear about you almost killing a member of staff, never mind breaking into the female ward?!"

I had never seen him emanate such rage. His muscles and veins visibly strained against his skin, and his eyes were so wide I could see the whites of them. That was when something shifted deep within him, and that evil presence I had sensed before returned with a vengeance.

Inhaling quick, shallow breaths to calm my panicked nerves, I ignored the pain in my jaw and assured, "I did **nothing**!"

"Then why were you found wearing his uniform?!" Doctor Hailey demanded, spittle now building up in the corners of his mouth.

"Because Randy told me to!" I admitted, and the violence glittering behind Doctor Hailey's dark, penetrating gaze abruptly vanished.

He was silent for a moment before wondering, "You don't mean Randall Emerson, do you?" But I didn't know the patient's surname.

Surely there aren't many Randy's here?

"I dunno..." I replied with a shrug, which I instantly regretted as my body ached, "Weird, creepy guy who says '**Ya get?**' a lot." My response triggered something as Doctor Hailey's animosity swiftly resurfaced.

"For fuck's sake!" He fumed, pounding a fist on the bed mere inches from my face, making me recoil.

"I **explicitly** told you to stay away from him!" He carried on in annoyance once he turned away, scrubbing both hands through his coiffed locks.

Curiosity overwhelmed me, and I couldn't help but ponder. *Why do I need to stay away from Randy?* But I knew now was not the time to ask questions, especially when I should already know the answers.

Once he had cooled down somewhat, Doctor Hailey turned to me and asked, "What happened?"
I then explained everything. When I had finished, he merely stared at me with wide, disbelieving eyes, unmoving from his spot beside me. *Isn't he gonna say anything?* Opening my mouth to prompt him, there was a sudden rapping at the door, distracting us.

"**Don't** say anything!" Doctor Hailey quietly growled before hollering, "What?!"
The clip-clop of heels echoed around the room when Nurse Deadman entered with papers in hand. *What's she doing here?*
"Here's Mr Moon's paperwork that you requested." She answered my unspoken thoughts.
Her horrid smile grew when she peered down at me with her stone-cold, blue eyes, as if quietly saying, '**You'll be coming with me soon.**'.

Flipping through the papers, Doctor Hailey wandered over to the desk, setting them down when he came to the last page. Stiffly leaning up on my elbows, I glanced over, hoping to take a peek at the papers, but I knew it was pointless; I couldn't make out a single word from where I was. An excruciating pain then flared up in my ribs, and I immediately slumped back down with a massive gasp.

"It's all there." Nurse Deadman assured, momentarily gaining Doctor Hailey's attention, who retrieved a pen clipped to his breast pocket.
What's all there? What is it? What's he about to sign? I needed to know and tried leaning up again to take a look; however, the suffering that coursed throughout my body was too much for me to bear.

Just as Doctor Hailey's pen tip touched the paper, he glanced at Nurse Deadman and asked, "And where's Mr Emerson's paperwork?"
His question brought her up short as she blurted in uncertainty, "What?"
"Mr Emerson's paperwork isn't here." He clarified, "His name also wasn't on the solitary confinement list like Mr Moon's, so that leads me to presume he's either in there without my prior approval, or his actions have been unduly overlooked, unlike Mr Moon's."

Silence filled the room, so quiet I would have heard a pin drop. *What's he doing?* I deliberated, staring from Doctor Hailey to Nurse Deadman, who looked like a deer caught in the headlights.

When she didn't reply, Doctor Hailey pressed, "I won't be signing anything until I have his paperwork."

He then pocketed his pen, a silent indication that he had made up his mind.

"But Mr Emerson didn't attack Ray!" Nurse Deadman proclaimed.

I opened my mouth to defend myself, but Doctor Hailey jumped to my rescue, "And how do you know that?"

"Because Mr Moon was wearing his uniform!" She pointed out smugly, as if it were absolute.

Unconvinced, Doctor Hailey retorted in an ominous undertone while slowly advancing on her, "You and I are both well aware of what Mr Emerson is capable of..." He trailed off, as if letting the solidity weigh down on her momentarily.

"**He** is in here for rape and murder whilst Mr Moon is not." He carried on, and I couldn't stop my jaw from dropping.

Wait, what?! Murder?! I gaped, horrified. *Then why the fuck are they letting him roam around with everyone?!*

"Nothing is certain until Ray wakes up." Doctor Hailey stated, dragging me back to the conversation, "Until then, they are both to be treated as suspects. So, if you want me to sign **this**..." And he gestured to the paperwork with a sweep of his hand, "Then I suggest you bring me Mr Emerson's."

He didn't give Nurse Deadman a chance to reply before ushering her out with a shooing motion, speaking to her like a dog, "Off you go."

She stared at him, dumbfounded, before leaving, clearly not used to being spoken to like that.

When the clip-clop of heels faded into the distance, Doctor Hailey turned on me and unexpectedly snapped, "You assured me you'd get the job done, but now look at you!" He gestured to my face with a sharp wave, "It's only a matter of time until Fred finds out who you are and what we're doing!"

Shocked by his sudden transformation from Doctor Jekyll to Mr Hyde, I couldn't hold Doctor Hailey's dark, penetrating gaze for a moment longer. My eyes flitted around the room, never settling on an object for too long. *If only I knew what was going on, then none of this would be happening!* I couldn't even ask, terrified of the outcome. *Would he think I'm crazy? Or crazier than what I'm meant to be?* Doctor Hailey must have sensed my apprehension as he placed a consoling hand on my shoulder, taking me aback. *And there he goes again, jumping from one persona to another...*

"Here's what we're going to do." He began, giving my shoulder a gentle squeeze and instantly making me uncomfortable, "Once Cora has returned with the paperwork and I've signed it, I'll explain that I'll return you to solitary confinement after your physical examination."

Hopefully, he'll give me something for the pain.

"I quickly picked up a camera from my office on the way here. All the footage has been transferred, and it's all charged and ready for you to use." Doctor Hailey continued, and I inwardly tensed at the mention of the camera.

I still haven't a clue what I'm meant to be doing!

"But we'll need to pick the other one up from your cell on the way to solitary confinement, then I can get that one charged and all footage removed."

I didn't know what to say, so I merely nodded. *Seriously, what the hell is going on?!*

Doctor Hailey then proceeded to check my battered and bruised body, fixing my busted nose before making sure nothing else was broken. After he had given me some painkillers, he began studying my eyesight, but there was a rapping at the door.

"Yes?!" He hollered, and I was consumed with trepidation when Nurse Deadman stepped inside with a wad of papers in her tight grasp.

"Here's Mr Emerson's paperwork that you requested." She commented sourly, reluctantly passing them to Doctor Hailey, who began thumbing through them.

Once satisfied, he retrieved his pen, signing mine and Randy's papers before returning them.

"I'll escort Mr Moon back to solitary confinement after his physical examination." He explained, shooing her out of the room again, "Now go."

"But, Doctor!" Nurse Deadman began heatedly, her features tightening in irritation, "He **isn't** your patient!"

"And neither is he yours." Doctor Hailey calmly retorted, a

darkness engulfing him, instantly putting her on edge.
"Now, I'd leave if I were you." He coldly added, "Unless you wish for me to issue you a written warning for questioning my authority." That comment had Nurse Deadman stiffen with consternation before she swiftly left without another word.

"We need to leave." Doctor Hailey abruptly commented once her footsteps had disappeared.
He then rummaged in his coat pocket, retrieving something small, black, and rectangular with a button-looking thing attached at the top. *What's that?* I deliberated before he leant across, reaching for my shirt. *Wait, what's he doing?!* I tried to shrink away when he unbuttoned my collar, but I had nowhere to go. Before I could say anything, he tucked the rectangular object down my shirt. *Wait, is this the camera?* I realised the button-looking thing was actually a lens but now acted as a buttonhole.

"We need to leave now." Doctor Hailey prompted again, standing straight and letting out a hiss.
"Cor, my back..." He griped, pressing a hand to his lower back before shaking off his obvious discomfort.
He then stiffly advanced on the door, but I could barely lean up on my elbows, never mind swing my legs around to sit on the edge of the bed. *Urgh... The painkillers haven't kicked in yet...*

However, I still tried to sit up, but a cry of pain broke my hold.
"I-I can't..." I rasped, slumping back onto the bed, "I-I just can't get up!"
Squeezing my eyes tightly shut, I gritted my teeth as the suffering refused to subside. I then felt Doctor Hailey's presence loom over me, so I immediately opened my eyes as I didn't like not knowing what he was doing.

"I can't give you any more medication, so what do you want? A wheelchair?" He queried, and I stoically replied, "You can carry me instead if you want."
I thought I saw a glimmer of amusement sparkle in his dark eyes, but it was gone before I could be sure.
"All right," He said, turning for the door, "I'll be back in a moment." And he left without another word.

Frustration consumed me as I lay there staring at the stark white ceiling. *If only these painkillers were working, then I could've used this opportunity to try and escape!* That thought alone had a tightness form in my chest. *I just want to get the hell outta here! I just want my life back!* Then the squeak of wheels echoed outside, making me realise I wouldn't have had time to leave without being seen.

The door opened with a gentle bang; I managed to peer down to see Doctor Hailey walk in backwards with a wheelchair, the wheels incessantly screeching. *God, that noise!* I cringed. He then turned around and pushed the chair over to me, positioning it so it was easy for him to help me down into it. Once comfortable, Doctor Hailey wheeled me towards the male ward. Not once did he utter a word, but I presumed that was because we often passed staff members, and he didn't want anyone to potentially overhear our conversation.

When we came to the gated entrance, he unexpectedly leaned down and whispered, "Remember, we need to find the camera before Fred comes looking for you." Just those words alone caused a shiver to creep up my spine.

But I don't know where it is! I inwardly declared, stretching my hands wide on the armrests before relaxing them again.

After he had locked the gate behind us, Doctor Hailey wheeled me down the eerily quiet hallway, stopping just outside a metal door along the left; it was a stone's throw from solitary confinement. *Is this it? Is this my cell?* I deliberated whilst he rummaged in his pocket, producing a set of keys that softly rattled.

But the silence was abruptly obliterated when he opened the door. The scraping of metal made me wince; I even covered my ears, but it still didn't drown out the noise. Doctor Hailey pulled the door to once he pushed me inside; the crack of light from the entrance sliced through the dreary room, identical to the one in the female ward.

"Where's the camera?" He instantly probed, peering around before circling his gaze back down to me.

At first, I didn't want to reply, knowing that foreboding presence about him would return with a vengeance. *But I don't know.* I admitted, my stomach churning as I shifted uncomfortably in the wheelchair.

After a moment of silence, Doctor Hailey urged, "Well? Where is it?"

I wetted my lips before replying in a slightly strained tone, "I... I dunno..."

"What do you mean you **don't know**?!" He shouted, frustrated, "How don't you know where you put the camera?!" *Because I'm not who you think I am!* I inwardly screamed, and my annoyance was evident in the heavy sigh that seeped from my lips.

"I don't understand what's wrong with you lately!" Doctor Hailey fumed while advancing to the closest bed, searching the pillow and bedsheet before repeating the same process on the other.

"It's as if someone has turned off the light and no one's home." He spoke with forced restraint, "You're like a different person now!" And he had hit the nail right on the head.

That's because I am a different person!

Angrily tossing the pillow back onto the bed, Doctor Hailey rounded on me and snapped, "Where is it, Rick?!"

It took every ounce of self-control to stop myself from retaliating. *I don't fucking know!* I wanted to scream. I wanted to drag him inside my head so he knew exactly what I was going through. *But I can't...* I sighed, all animosity dissipating. *So I may as well try and figure out where this camera is...*

Once I had quietly evaluated the room, I peered over at Doctor Hailey and suggested, "Have you tried the bedframe?"

"The bedframe?" He repeated with a furrowed brow, checking the right one to no avail.

As he wandered back over to the other, he grumbled under his breath, "How doesn't he know where his Goddamn camera is?!" He then knelt, but a groan of pain leaked from his lips, causing him to rest against the bed for a moment. *Is it his back again?*

Once he regained himself, Doctor Hailey searched the bedframe in annoyance.

"If you've lost it," He heatedly began, "I'll be having words with your-" But he cut himself off when he pulled his hand free, a camera now in his grasp.

Wait, what was he about to say? I got the distinct feeling he was going to tell me more information about who I was meant to be.

Shaking his head, Doctor Hailey stiffly rose to his feet, using the bed as an aid.

"Why couldn't you have just told me it was there in the first place?" He asked, but I didn't know what to tell him.

I can't tell him that it was just a guess!

"Well?!" He sharply urged.

His dark eyes were cold and flinty as he stared ominously at me, implanting in me a fear that was on par with Doctor Sasin's. *There's something about this guy I don't trust or like...* But I couldn't put my finger on what.

"**RICK!**" Doctor Hailey abruptly barked, making me flinch, "What's the matter with you recently?!"

I tried to keep my mouth shut but couldn't take the barrage of questions anymore, so in the heat of the moment, I just blurted, "I don't remember, okay?!"

I was quietly surprised when his menacing aura vanished, replaced with an indescribable concern.

After a moment of silence, Doctor Hailey queried, "You don't remember?"

I shouldn't have said anything! I scolded, averting my gaze in fear his Hyde side would return.

"That explains so much..." He murmured more to himself, gaining my attention as he repeatedly rubbed his face.

When his dark eyes caught me staring, he shifted his attention back to me and commented, "It must be because of your sessions with Fred."

Pocketing the camera, Doctor Hailey added, "The sooner we get the evidence, the sooner all of this will be over and done with."

Again, what evidence is he on about? I wanted to ask but knew I couldn't. I was lucky he had readily accepted my excuse about the camera's whereabouts. *He may not be as understanding next time...*

Once he had opened the door and turned the wheelchair around, Doctor Hailey pushed me back out into the corridor, locking the cell behind us. I could hear an assortment of voices coming from solitary confinement as we advanced towards it, but the one I immediately recognised was the hoarse tone of Doctor Sasin. *What's he gonna do to me today?!* Fear gripped me like a vice; I honestly thought my heart was going to explode out of my chest when we were granted access by the guard.

"Ahhh, there's **my** patient!" Doctor Sasin's voice reverberated down the hallway, and in that split second, a cold sweat consumed me.

I wanted to flee. I wanted to hide as a sense of impending doom washed over me when I spotted him standing outside my assigned room.

"Leave him there." Doctor Sasin advised, raising his hand when Doctor Hailey wheeled me towards him, "I'll take him to the therapy room once Nurse Deadman has returned."

No, no, no, not another session! My heart palpitations caused a tingling in my chest. *I can't do this! I can't go through another session!* Doctor Hailey must have sensed my inner turmoil as he placed a consoling hand on my shoulder, giving it a gentle squeeze.

His dark gaze then circled to Doctor Sasin, wondering, "Is that necessary, Fred?"

Doctor Sasin opened his mouth to reply but was distracted by the clunk of metal from the gated entrance behind Doctor Hailey and me.

"Perfect timing!" He gleamed when Nurse Deadman and her two puppy-dog orderlies appeared with Randy in their grasp.

What's he doing here? I mulled before remembering Doctor Hailey had requested his paperwork.

"Doc, what 'ave I done wrong?" Randy questioned when he was pulled to a halt just in front of Doctor Sasin, having to tip his head back to stare up at him, "Why the fuck am I 'ere?"

A sly smirk pulled at the corner of Doctor Sasin's lips when he replied, "You can thank him for that." And he gestured over at me with a nod.

Wait, what?! I gawked, hastily averting my gaze when Randy's cunning blue eyes locked onto me; such rage danced within that I honestly thought he could kill me with looks alone.

Jabbing a finger in my face, Randy vowed, "Yer'll regret this!"

I still refused to look at him until he was dragged away toward a cell Doctor Sasin had unlocked directly opposite mine.

"Mark my fuckin' words, Trav!" He gutturally carried on, his lips pulled back and baring his rotten and cracked teeth, "Yer'll fuckin' regret makin' an enemy outta me!"

Chapter Eight

He knows!

"Right, Richard," Doctor Sasin began, entwining his fingers on his desk to gain my attention.

I was strapped to the gas chamber chair directly opposite him, with Stallone and Schwarzenegger standing guard on either side whilst Nurse Deadman lingered beside his desk.

An overpowering sense of alarm encompassed me; I knew exactly where this conversation was going. *And if I don't say what he wants to hear, then he's gonna take me straight back to the therapy room!* Just the thought of another session made me choke, as if someone were smothering me. *But I haven't a clue what he's on about!*

"Have we learned a valuable lesson yet?" Doctor Sasin continued, and those words alone ignited a deep, enrooted fear I had been harbouring.

Just say what he wants to hear! I urged as a cold sweat consumed me. *Just say what he wants to hear!* But I couldn't as my breaths were now bursting in and out, my heart beating so fast it made my chest hurt. *JUST SAY WHAT HE WANTS TO HEAR!*

"Don't make me have to ask again..." Doctor Sasin threatened, and that was enough for my fear to mutate into terror.

An unexpected dizzy spell crashed over me, swiftly accompanied by black dots that wouldn't disappear no matter how many times I blinked. *I need to breathe! I need to breathe!* I chanted over and over when I started to hyperventilate, but it was all to no avail as vivid memories now flashed through my head like a stun grenade. I tried to make them go away by squeezing my eyes tightly shut, but before I could open them, I was bombarded by a medicinal smell that now lingered in the atmosphere. *Not real! Not real!* Cold metal was suddenly pressed against my back. ***NOT REAL!*** But it was hard to convince myself when fingers pried open my mouth, shoving something wooden inside.

My eyes snapped open, and I was greeted by the imposing figure of Doctor Sasin leering over me. I screamed in fear, but it was muffled by the wooden peg in my mouth. *This* ***can't*** *be real!* I was now lying on a metal bed in the therapy room. *This is just a dream!* But I doubted myself as his hoarse voice sounded too real to be a dream.

"Have we learned a valuable lesson yet?" Doctor Sasin queried, producing two crude head electrodes from the trolley beside him; I couldn't reply even if I wanted to.

Wake up! Just wake the hell up! I wailed as he fastened them on either side of my head. *It's just a dream!* But it felt more like a nightmare when a wave of electricity shot through my brain, causing my body to involuntarily jerk and shake. ***NO MORE!*** I frightfully shrieked, swiftly closing my eyes once the current had passed; relieved darkness now embraced me.

"No more what?" The recognisable voice of Doctor Sasin wondered, and that was when I became acutely aware I was sat upright once more.

Blinking open my eyes, I stared around the office and then down at the gas chamber chair I was still strapped to. *What... What the fuck just happened?...*

"No more what?!" Doctor Sasin stridently urged, distracting me. *Wait, what did he just say?* It then dawned on me I must have accidentally spoken aloud. *Shit!*

Choosing to keep my thoughts to myself, I hastily averted my gaze, "Nuh-Nothing..." I nervously stammered.

"Well, I hope that's your way of agreeing you have learned your lesson." He retorted with narrowed eyes and a fake smile, "I don't expect to have words with you again about attacking **my** staff."

It suddenly became crystal clear why he had been tormenting me for days. *All this because he* ***thinks*** *I attacked that orderly?!* My nervousness abruptly vanished, replaced with acrimony. *When will it sink into that thick skull of his that I did* ***nothing*** *wrong?!* The more I seethed, the more I couldn't rein in the rage bubbling within me like a volcano ready to erupt.

Now I had reached my boiling point, I no longer cared about the consequences of my actions as Doctor Sasin had ignited my volatile nature.

Without much thought, I gutturally roared, "**I DIDN'T FUCKING ATTACK HIM, RANDY DID!**" And my outburst clearly took him aback by his wide eyes and slack mouth.

The orderlies on either side then clenched their hands into fists, as if ready to beat me to a bloody pulp, but Doctor Sasin stopped them with a brief raise of his hand.

"I'd shut your mouth if I were you, Mr Moon!" Doctor Sasin coldly threatened, but this time, he didn't manage to get under my skin, and I furiously snapped back, "YOU **WILL** FUCKING LISTEN TO ME!"

Much to my surprise, no one said anything, and now I had everyone's undivided attention; I calmly explained, "Randy was the one who attacked him, smashed his face against the wall, and then told me to get changed into his uniform."

Once I had finished, Doctor Sasin's deadpan façade returned, but there was no denying the underlying anger by his cold, flinty eyes, which practically burnt a hole through me.

"I will **not** have you accuse patients of your ungodly actions!" He fumed with a slightly raised, shaky voice, and I heatedly retorted, "But **you're** accusing me!"

My factious reply had his features unexpectedly crack once more; carnal violence glowered back at me when he exploded, "**BECAUSE YOU WERE THE ONE WEARING BLOODSTAINED CLOTHES, NOT RANDALL!**"

At that moment, when I saw Doctor Sasin's true colours show through his usual detached exterior, I knew he would literally kill me if I didn't keep my mouth shut. Even Nurse Deadman looked slightly shaken by his outburst when she sidestepped away, clearly uncomfortable being too close to him.

Doctor Sasin must have clocked how unsettled everyone was as his impassive attitude swiftly reappeared.

"Richard..." He began with a slight shake of his head, "I'm just a little upset as I thought we had made progress..."

He was contemplative for a moment before an unkind smile slowly spread across his sculpted face; a wild-eyed gaze stared back at me.

"I'll tell you what," He insidiously said, "We'll put you out of your misery today by... Trying... Something more-"

"Aggressive?" I presumed, and my comment made him chuckle unpleasantly.

"Permanent." He corrected.

"Wait, what?!" I hawked, shocked, "What do you mean '**permanent**'?"

He didn't get the chance to respond as the rotary-dial telephone rattled to life on his desk: **RING, RING! RING, RING!** Doctor Sasin's glacial blue eyes momentarily shifted to the phone before over at Nurse Deadman.

"Answer that for me." He instructed while rising to his feet, advancing on the orderlies.

"Of course, Doctor." Nurse Deadman enthusiastically nodded, leaning across to pick it up, "Merriwell Sanatorium. Nurse Deadman speaking. How may I help you?"

"I want you both to take Mr Moon straight down to the infirmary." Doctor Sasin informed Stallone and Schwarzenegger when he stood before them, "Deadman and I shall be along shortly to prep him for surgery."

SURGERY?! I gaped. *What the fuck is he gonna do with me?!*

"What surgery?" I asked, but he didn't reply, as if I hadn't uttered a word at all.

No, they're not prepping me for anything until I know what the fuck's going on!

"What surgery?!" I demanded, undeterred, but Doctor Sasin continued to ignore me while the orderlies unfastened the straps around my arms.

*He **will** answer me!*

I opened my mouth to snap, but Nurse Deadman quickly piped up, "Doctor, it's the hospital."

Doctor Sasin's attention shifted to her as she added, "Ray's finally awake." She then held out the receiver, gesturing for him to take it.

Now perched on the edge of his desk, Doctor Sasin snatched the phone from her and pressed it to his ear.

"Does he remember what happened?!" He brusquely asked.

By now, I had been hoisted to my feet, unable to find the physical strength to fight as my whole body sang with unchecked pain from all the sessions and beatings. *What the hell is he gonna do with me?!* I panicked when the orderlies lugged me towards the door, my shoes shrieking against the floorboards like a dissonant caterwaul. Then I heard the clip-clop of heels before Nurse Deadman appeared, about to open the door, but Doctor Sasin stopped her with a click of his fingers, his hand raised, gesturing for us to wait.

"I see..." He quietly muttered down the phone, shaking his head in frustration, "Thank you for finding out. I'll make sure either myself or Elon visit him tonight."

He hung up without another word, weaving his hands through his hair, pulling on it slightly. *What's been said?* I fretted, unable to ignore the disappointment gracing his sculpted face.

After a moment of silence, Doctor Sasin rose to his feet and spoke directly to the orderlies, "Take Mr Moon straight to the recreation room."

Wait, what, why?! I was so confused. *What the hell's been said?! Why's he changed his mind?!*

"Deadman," He carried on, briefly covering his face with his hands, "You're coming with me to solitary confinement. I need to have a word with Mr Emerson."

His glacial blue eyes shifted to me, and I instantly knew why he had changed his mind. *He was told I didn't attack that orderly.*

Once Doctor Sasin had ushered everyone out and locked the office door behind him, the orderlies dragged me down to the recreation room. An old black-and-white movie was playing obnoxiously loud.

"We'll be keeping a close eye on you!" Stallone threatened before wandering off to stand guard by the exit with Schwarzenegger.

I didn't know what to do with myself, and there was no way I could escape without someone noticing. *Besides, I can't risk pissing Doctor Sasin off...* I had no idea what he had intended to do with me, but I wasn't willing to find out.

Advancing on the chairs facing the movie, I went to sit down but froze when someone squealed my name, "RIIIIICKY!" I instantly recognised the annoying, singsong voice.

Urgh... What does he want?... I inwardly groaned when I spotted Adi waving at me like a madman. He was sitting on the sofa that had its back to the film. He then frantically beckoned me over, looking like one of those waving cats you would see in the local Chinese takeaway but on speed.

"RIIIIIIIIICKY!" He hollered again, gaining the attention of nearby patients desperately trying to watch the film.
"You can show me how to play poker!" He obliviously carried on. I was about to turn him down before realising. *He'll just keep going on and on until I give in...* So I begrudgingly trudged over and sat down on the sofa opposite, noticing he already had the cards in hand.

"What was it?" Adi abruptly queried, shuffling the deck with such expertise that I would have thought he had once worked in a casino, "Three?"
Shaking my head, I corrected, "No, you deal two."
He tossed two cards face down in my direction, his hazel-coloured eyes fixated on me. *What's he looking at?* His eyes didn't quite reach my gaze, peering at something off-centre.
"What?" I blurted as Adi set the deck aside, "What you looking at?"

Still staring, he asked, "How was shock therapy?"
I then realised he had been looking at the burns on my temples all along. I didn't know what to say. His bluntness stunned me, so I averted my gaze and glanced at anything but him. *What does he expect me to say? That I had a fun fucking time?*

"Also," Adi began, not continuing until I fixed my sights back upon him, "You forgot the '**are**'. What **are** you looking at?"
I wasn't sure if he was being serious or making light of the conversation. *I just never know with this guy...*
Forcing a hard smile, I bitterly replied, "Thanks for the English lesson..."
He didn't grasp my sarcasm as he delightfully gleamed, "Anytime, bestest bud!"
*He does realise '**bestest**' isn't a word, right?*

"So, I heard you killed an orderly, stole his clothes, and snuck into the female ward." Adi rambled, picking his cards up to look at them, which irked me.
No, no, no, he shouldn't have turned them over- Then I realised what he had said. *Wait, what?!* I immediately drew my head back in shock, a heavy feeling growing in the pit of my stomach when his words finally sunk in. *Is that what everyone thinks? That I killed someone?*

"Was it worth it?" Adi softly carried on, shuffling forward to sit on the edge of his seat.
Ignoring his question, I snapped, "I didn't kill anyone!"

"But you snuck into the female ward?" He probed, continuing before I could explain myself, "Why?"
That fateful day then came crashing over me. I remembered how desperate I was to talk to Jack that I risked the life of another. *I should **never** have trusted Randy!* But hindsight did very little to change my regrets.
I then realised Adi was still staring expectantly at me, so I reluctantly stated, "I just needed to talk to Jack..."

'Please tell me you've at least spoken to Jack and Adi!'. Doctor Hailey's voice abruptly came to mind, and I was suddenly lost amidst my curious thoughts. *Why do I need to talk to them?* I mulled, gazing at Adi with unanticipated focus. *What's so special about them?* ***'You did get the evidence, didn't you?'***. Doctor Hailey's question infiltrated my deliberations. ***'You were wearing the camera, weren't you?'***. Then his comment from the other day when we were in the infirmary flashed across my mind. ***'It's only a matter of time until Fred finds out who you are and what we're doing!'***. *If this is all to do with Doctor Sasin, what do Jack and Adi know?...* I wondered with a curious tip of my head, a desire to uncover the truth now gnawing away deep within me.

Before Adi could pipe up, I hastily blurted, "You're Doctor Sasin's patient, right?"
His eyebrows squished together in confusion before he nodded once.
"What exactly is he treating you for?" I pried, leaning forward with great intrigue, "Why are you here?" And I immediately regretted asking; anguish now graced his face.
Adi scrubbed a hand around the back of his neck, his teeth audibly grinding. His shoulders curled forward, trying to make himself as small as possible. *What the hell did I say?* Worried, I repeatedly rubbed my face while watching him deal with his inner turmoil.

I need to say something. I realised when he started visibly sweating, so I leaned across the table and placed a consoling hand on his leg.
"Hey," I spoke softly, not continuing until his eyes locked onto mine, "What's wrong?"
His visible suffering then contorted into shame.
Unable to hold my gaze, Adi quietly muttered, "How do I tell him? And if I do, what will he think of me now?"

He then crumpled onto the sofa, releasing an uncontrollable moan that gained a few nearby patients' attention. *What the hell did he do?*

The crackling of static then echoed around the recreation room; I had no idea where the noise was coming from until I clocked several speakers fastened to the walls.

"Staff announcement!" The venomous voice of Nurse Deadman blared through the speakers, making me realise it was a public address system.

"Can doctors Hailey, Bueter, Scandura, and Kröger please head straight to solitary confinement in the male ward! That's doctors Hailey, Bueter, Scandura, and Kröger to head straight to solitary confinement in the male ward!"

Then the crackling abruptly stopped; all I could hear now was the obnoxiously loud movie still playing. *What was all that abo-*

"If I tell you," Adi began panickily, firmly grasping his shoulders to try and still his quaking body, "You've got to promise not to tell anyone!"

A tightness formed in my chest as I stared at him; I couldn't help but apprehensively wonder. *Did... Did he... Kill someone?...* But I couldn't believe it; I refused to believe it. *He wouldn't hurt a fly!* But then I started to doubt myself. *What other reason could it be if he's so scared to tell me?*

"I... I promise..." I reluctantly replied, but even I could hear the unease underlying my voice; Adi either hadn't noticed or chose to ignore it.

Gripping his hands together, he wetted his lips before quietly admitting, "I'm... I'm gay..."

Once his words had sunk in, I couldn't help but blurt in disbelief, "What?"

He's gay?... Thinking back over the way he acted, I wasn't surprised. *Not that I had given it much thought...* I was still confused as to why he was ashamed. *Who cares if he likes men?*

Taken aback, Adi questioned, "Is that all you've got to say?" It felt as if he weren't happy with my response, so much so that he anxiously said, "Aren't you disgusted? Disappointed? Anything?"

Shaking my head, I earnestly replied, "Why would I care if you're gay?" But he still didn't believe me by the impatient snort expelled from him.

"So, is that why you're here?" I queried, ignoring his evident frustration, "Because you're gay?"

"**SSSSHHHH!**" Adi hushed urgently, frantically waving his hands for me to be quiet while staring around with wide eyes; clearly terrified someone may have overheard.

Once he had checked, double-checked, and triple-checked that no one was paying attention to us, he turned to me and said bluntly, "Yes."

But why?

The curiosity on my face must have been a dead giveaway as Adi reluctantly explained with a sigh, "It's my fault... My family are very, **very** religious, yet I still told them..."

His eyes turned downcast, and a pained expression consumed his features, which he quickly hid by scrubbing a hand across his face.

"I guess I hoped they would accept me... But deep down, I should've known better..."

He then lowered his hand and squeezed his eyes tightly shut.

"They told me to pray to God for forgiveness and to steer me back onto the correct path, but no amount of praying can change who I am..."

Slowly, Adi opened his eyes but refused to look at me, clearly ashamed of his actions.

He then crossed his arms over his stomach, as if in a protective huddle, before carrying on, "When they realised I was a lost cause, they made an appointment here to speak to someone about my condition, but the doctor refused to admit me for something that wasn't an illness."

"Then why are you here?" I curiously wondered, furrowing my brow.

Adi finally locked his eyes on mine when he professed, "Because Doctor Sasin got involved. He said he would take me in as a patient if they paid him every month under the table until I was cured." He then stared around in defeat, adding with a broken smile, "And here I am six years later..."

Is that why Doctor Hailey wants his help? To prove Doctor Sasin is treating someone without due cause? Then my mind drifted to Jack. *Why's she here, and what does she know?* That thought alone had me focus back on Adi. *Perhaps he has an idea.*

Now Adi had finished, I forced a smile and said, "Well, don't stop being you." And his anxieties visibly fizzled away, relief now gracing his face.

"And that's why you're my bestest bud!" He exclaimed in delight.

Yeeeah, but I'm not... I awkwardly pondered. *He thinks I'm someone else...*

"Anyway," I swiftly changed the subject, "Do you know why Jack's here? Is she also one of Doctor Sasin's patients?"

Adi's brow scrunched up in confusion when he pressed, "Why are you asking about Jack?"

His lack of forthcoming made my stomach harden in frustration.

Why's he being so cagey about Jack when he just told me one of his biggest secrets?

I shook my head and cupped my hands, begging, "**Please!** Just answer me, and I'll explain everything." But I had no idea what exactly I was going to tell him.

I just need to know so I can piece everything together. Until then, everything was just a guessing game.

Narrowing his eyes in suspicion, Adi was thoughtful for a moment before countering, "Everything?"

I was initially a little taken aback before nodding, "Everything."

Well... As much as I know, anyway...

Again, he considered what I said before abruptly holding out his hand with a broad smile, exclaiming, "Deal!"

He then leant across, grasping mine before I could react, giving it a surprisingly firm shake.

Once Adi had released my hand, he finally answered my questions, "I don't exactly know why Jack's here. I've heard rumours that she murdered her family, but she was found not guilty because of insanity."

Wait, there's another murderer?! A slight chill came over me.

How many people are in here for murder?

Feeling a little uneasy, I cleared my throat and repeated, "'**Murdered**'?..." But Adi seemed unfazed, so I tacked on, "Do you think she did it?"

Shrugging, he replied, "I don't even know if it's true."

So, she could be in here without reason as well? It all started to make sense why Doctor Hailey wanted help from these two. *But what's Doctor Sasin got to do with Jack if the judge sent her here?*

Sliding forward until I was perched on the edge of the sofa, I asked quietly, "Was Doctor Sasin paid to take her on as a patient as well?"

"No..." Adi murmured sceptically, a tightness forming in his face when he added, "I thought everyone knew he treated all the female patients?"

He does? I mulled, shocked.

"Why?" I immediately probed, hoping to get all the nitty-gritty information now he was more forthcoming.

Adi didn't get the chance to reply as someone suddenly towered over us.

"We need to leave!" The newcomer urgently declared, and I peered upwards to see Doctor Hailey.

Whoa! I gaped, unable to stop my jaw from dropping. *What happened to him?!* It was his broken nose I spotted first; fresh blood glistened from his nostrils. Then I saw the bruising coming out under his dark, penetrating eyes. *Has he been in a fight?* I clocked his split bottom lip; a trickle of dried blood trailed down his chin. I couldn't imagine him going fist-to-fist with someone, but I couldn't deny his strength whenever he dragged me somewhere. *Then the question is **who** has he been fighting?*

"Did you not hear me?!" Doctor Hailey snapped, dragging me back to the conversation, "We need to leave!"

Wait, leave?! I repeated, drawing my head back in apparent shock. *Why? What's going on?* Before I could question him, Doctor Hailey snatched me up by the front of my shirt, hoisting me to my feet.

"**NOW!**" He barked, "We need to leave now!" Then his eyes circled to Adi, "You're coming with us as well!"

Once Adi jumped up, Doctor Hailey immediately made a beeline for the hallway. *What the hell's going on?!* He then came to an abrupt halt by the doorway where two nurses and an orderly were lingering.

"I thought I told you to take the patients straight to their cells!" He fumed, his teeth bared in anger, yet his voice had an underlying sense of urgency.

Something isn't right... I muttered, my stomach quivering with unease. Without another word, Doctor Hailey left the recreation room with Adi and me hot on his heels.

"What the hell's going on?" I queried, but Doctor Hailey didn't reply as we hurried toward the female ward, "And where

are we goin-"
The wailing of a siren then sliced through the asylum, so piercing I wanted to slap my hands over my ears. Red lights now flashed throughout the building, illuminating the once-white walls forebodingly.

Undeterred, Doctor Hailey continued onwards through the gated entrance until we came to stand outside a cell door; all the while, nurses were ushering a small handful of female patients into their rooms. *Isn't this Jack's cell?* My suspicions were confirmed when he unlocked the metal door. Light from the hallway seeped inside, bathing Jack's face, who was sitting on the left bed, looking like a deer caught in the headlights.

"Out!" Doctor Hailey ordered, pointing at Jack with a trembling index finger.
She was hesitant at first until he barked, "**NOW!**"
She speedily rose to her feet, hurrying out into the hallway with her cellmate following. *Who's she?...* I murmured, peering at the cellmate in question.

Slapping a hand down onto the doorframe once Jack was out, Doctor Hailey prevented the cellmate from leaving. "Not you." He bluntly said, "I don't need you."
He then shunted her back inside, and she collapsed onto the bed, giving him time to lock the door.

"Follow me!" He urged, turning on his heels and rushing toward the gated entrance, leaving Jack, Adi, and me staring after him for a heartbeat.
Once we had caught up, Jack implored, "What the fuck's happening?!" Then she clocked his face, "And what the fuck happened to you?!"
He was silent, almost deep in thought, as he led us past the reception area. *Where's he taking us?!*

We charged through the male ward toward the far gated entry, uproarious screams echoing from solitary confinement. *What the hell's going on?!* But I didn't dare take a look. While Doctor Hailey unlocked the gate, torturous cries reverberated down the corridor to our right, which led to the therapy rooms. *Come on, come on, come on!* I urged, swallowing a lump that had formed in my throat. I tried to still my shaky hands when the cries drew closer, almost honing in on us from every angle. *Come on, hurry up!*

A wave of relief washed over me when Doctor Hailey finally unlocked the gate, ushering us toward the stairwell only to stop by the fire exit door. He tried to open it, but it wouldn't budge. Undiscouraged, he shouldered into it, but something blocked it from the other side.

"Fuck it..." He muttered under his breath with a shake of his head, clearly frustrated.

What now? I wondered before he stalked up the stairs, taking them two at a time. *Where's he going?*

We barely had the chance to follow before Doctor Hailey barked over his shoulder, "Hurry up!"

By now, he had reached the top and opened the door, only to jump back with a gasp when an orderly barged past. The orderly rushed down the stairs without even giving us a second glance. In the split second I saw the orderly's face; there was no denying the fear etched across it. *What the hell's he running from?*

Once the orderly had gone, Doctor Hailey beckoned us up the stairs and through the door. It was surprisingly quiet up here compared to down below, but I was still anxious to know what that orderly had been running from. *There's no one else up here!* Or at least I didn't think there was. We then sped along the hallway towards Doctor Hailey's office. He hastily unlocked it and hurried us inside with a frantic wave of his hand.

"Quickly, quickly, get in!" He pressed.

"Now, are you gonna tell us what the fuck's going on?" Jack questioned once Doctor Hailey slammed the door shut and locked it; I wasn't surprised he ignored her again.

"You need to talk to us!" I insisted as he darted behind his desk, picking up the telephone.

A look of defeat now graced his hatchet face as he slammed the receiver down, grumbling, "Damn it! He's cut the lines!"

Uncharacteristically, Doctor Hailey was quiet for a moment. *Why isn't he talking to us?!* His Adam's apple notably bobbed before he fumbled in his trouser pocket, producing a key to unlock one of his desk drawers.

"For fuck's sake!" Jack lost her temper, her jaw clenching in annoyance, "What the fuck's going on?! What's with all the lights?! The siren?! The-" But she faltered when Doctor Hailey produced a gun from the drawer.

What the hell's he gonna do with that?! Just the sight of the hardware made my heart race, beating ferociously against my chest. A shrill scream then escaped Adi, who anxiously hid behind me, gripping the back of my shirt and pulling it taut.

Gesturing with my hands for Doctor Hailey to calm down when he turned the gun to me, I desperately exclaimed, "Whoa, whoa! Just... Just take it easy, okay?!"

Oblivious to my consternation, Doctor Hailey unexpectedly said, "Here." And he shook the gun, urging me to take it.

Wait, what?! Stunned, I slowly blinked at the hardware still in his grasp. *Why's he giving it to me?...* Then he rummaged in the drawer with his free hand, retrieving something that looked like a passport.

When I made no move to take the weapon, Doctor Hailey growled, "Rick, take your Goddamn gun!" That comment brought me up short.

Wait, ***my*** *gun?!* A knot formed in my stomach the longer I stared at it. *But I don't even know how to use one!* I couldn't reach for it even if I wanted to; my arms were limp, hanging like deadweight by my sides. **BANG!** Doctor Hailey slammed the drawer shut, making Adi flinch, who now clung to me like a baby monkey.

"Take your fucking gun!" Doctor Hailey bellowed as he stormed around his desk, ramming the gun so hard into my chest it made an oof escape me.

I barely caught it before he shoved the passport-looking thing into my palms, my hands fumbling to ensure I didn't drop them. *What the hell's this?* I mulled, glimpsing at the passport, surprised when I realised what it was. *Why's he given me this?...* Opening it, I saw a metal badge and the police ID card; a photo of me stared back.

Then it dawned on me. *No, I... I* ***can't*** *be a cop!* I proclaimed with a vigorous shake of my head, refusing to believe it. Just staring at my photo ID – *Which* ***can't*** *be me as my name isn't Richard!* – was like a massive slap to the face, a reminder I had let my family down. *It's what Nanna wanted me to be...* My dad and grandad were police officers. *So it was expected of me to follow in their footsteps...*

"Now do you understand the urgency?!" Doctor Hailey implored, his voice breaking as panic set in, "He knows!" That sentence made a shiver creep up my spine; I knew exactly who

he was referring to.
But how are we gonna get out of here?! The fire exit was blocked, and I doubted the main entrance was open.
"Fred will kill you if he gets his hands on you, all because you let it slip in front of Randy that we're working together!" Doctor Hailey quickly added, dragging me back to the conversation, "So we need to leave before it's too late!"

His dark, penetrating gaze then shifted to Jack and Adi, and I knew he needed them on his side for the evidence he so desperately wanted.
"I need you both to testify against Doctor Sasin." Doctor Hailey started, his gaze settling on Jack, "For sexual assault..." And then he shifted to Adi, "And for fraud by abuse of position..." He then looked at me for confirmation, "If you do, Rick will ensure your freedom."
Will I?... I was taken aback but merely nodded, wanting to escape this hellhole before Doctor Sasin found us.

"What about a clean slate?" Jack pried, peering over at me questioningly.
I was shocked and didn't know what to say. *I don't even know if that's something I can do...*
I knew I needed to tell her what she wanted to hear, so I nodded and said, "We'll iron out the finer details later."

"So that's all settled?" Doctor Hailey queried, peering between Jack and Adi, who nodded in agreement.
A slow smile spread across his hatchet face before he nodded toward the door, "Then let's go!"

Chapter Nine

I vill schoot you!

"Where we going now?" Jack inquired while insufferable screams echoed from somewhere down below, chilling me to my very core.

What the hell's going on?! I fretted as we bolted toward the stairwell, my mouth so dry it would put the Sahara Desert to shame.

"It's '**are**'. Where **are** we going now." Adi corrected, clearly annoying Jack judging by the twitch underneath her left eye.

"Now isn't the time for a grammar lesson!" Doctor Hailey scolded, evidently just as irritated.

His frustration vanished when his dark, penetrating gaze momentarily locked onto Jack, answering, "And there's a way out through the church."

"The church?" I repeated as Doctor Hailey ripped open the stairwell door, hurrying us through with a wave of his hand. "Then why didn't we head straight there after getting Jack?" I added as we rushed down the stairs, our footsteps resonating off the walls like timpani drums.

Once we reached the bottom, he bluntly explained, "Because I don't know who will be in there, so I'd rather you're armed than be completely defenceless."

He then glimpsed at the gun still in my grasp. *But I don't know how to use this!* Without another word, Doctor Hailey opened the door. The sound of tormented cries increased tenfold, making me flinch as they not only pierced my ears but also my heart. *It sounds like people are dying.*

"We need to hurry!" He urged, stepping out into the corridor, "It'll only be a matter of time before-"

"Doctoooooor Haaaaaaaileeeeeeey..." A deep, otherworldly voice drifted towards us like a storm on the wind.

Who the-

"Get your gun ready!" Doctor Hailey exhorted, pulling me in front of him so I faced the hallway leading to the therapy rooms.

"But-" I began just as metal suddenly shrieked over the screams and siren, the sound so shuddersome it was as if someone had dragged their nails across a chalkboard.

"GET YOUR GUN OUT NOW!" Doctor Hailey bellowed when a masculine figure loomed ahead; I could hardly make them out due to the flashing red lights.

Whoever he was just stood there for a moment, as if we were in a Mexican standoff; all the while, Doctor Hailey shouted for me to shoot him. A split second must have passed before the figure rushed down the corridor towards us, lugging something metal that scraped along the floor beside him.

"**GET UPSTAIRS!**" Doctor Hailey panicked, shoving us all through the doorway.

"You won't feel a thing!" That blood-chilling voice loomed hauntingly close, "I proooomiiiiiii-" But he was cut off when the door slammed shut behind us.

Who the fuck was that?! I fretted as we bolted up the stairs, trying to escape whoever had scared Doctor Hailey. *And I don't think he's the sort of person to scare easy...*

Once we reached the top, Doctor Hailey yanked open the door and charged over to the closest office, tugging the handle, but it wouldn't budge.

"Fuck it..." He cursed under his breath, his attention shifting to us, "Check the other doors!"

Adi inspected the next one, but that was also closed. *Why doesn't he unlock it? Or why don't we just go back to his office?* I could only put it down to a time factor.

"This one's unlocked!" Jack hollered before disappearing inside, so we all sprinted over just as the stairwell door opened with an almighty bang.

"Get in, get in!" Doctor Hailey urged, pushing Adi and me inside just as that blood-chilling voice drifted along the corridor, "You can't hide forever!"

Maniacal laughter swiftly followed before Doctor Hailey shut the door. Pressing an index finger to his lips, he pointed at the desk in the middle of the room before returning to the door, a silent gesture for us to block it. While Jack and I quickly but quietly moved the desk, Doctor Hailey locked the door.

"Who was that?" Adi queried with a tilt of his head, and everyone shushed him in unison as footsteps drew nearer.

"Come out, come out, whereveeer yooou aaaaare..." That blood-chilling voice cooed, heading in the direction of Doctor Hailey's office.

Is that why he didn't want to go back there? I deliberated, peering at Doctor Hailey, who was staring anxiously at the door. *Because whoever that is out there knows which one his office is?*

BANG! BANG! *What the hell's he doing out there?* I wasn't sure, but it sounded like a door was being shouldered into. **BANG!** *Thinking about it, why does he want Doctor Hailey so-* **SMASH!** Whatever he was barging into hit the floor with a crash; I presumed he had managed to bulldoze into Doctor Hailey's office.

A moment of silence followed before he gutturally roared, "**WHERE THE FUCK ARE YOU?!**"

The thud of furniture being upturned then vibrated throughout the walls.

"What now?" I whispered to Doctor Hailey, who had a fist pressed against his lips.

Lowering his hand, he uttered, "I... I don't know..."

He then wandered toward the window along the back wall while that guy shouted obscenities in the hallway. *How are we gonna get out of here?!* I worried, my gaze flitting around the room but never settling on anyone or anything for long.

There must be another way out of... My thoughts trailed off when I clocked the barred window Doctor Hailey was lingering beside. *Of course! The bars!*

Rushing over, I asked in a hushed tone, "What about the bars?"

Doctor Hailey was putting his nose back into place when he peered at me in confusion, asking, "What about them?"

CRACK! I couldn't help but grimace when he casually realigned it, as if it hadn't hurt.

"Is there any way we can get them off?" I suggested, and that was when I saw the cogs furiously turn in his head.

After a brief moment, he wondered, "What would you need?"
"Well, a hacksaw should work." I proposed.
Nodding slowly, he mulled, "We may have one in the maintenance room downstairs, or at least something to bend-"
An ear-piercing scream sliced through the atmosphere, causing the hairs on the nape of my neck to rise. *Who the hell was that?!*

In the blink of an eye, Doctor Hailey was leant across the desk blocking the door, listening intently to the commotion outside. Hurrying over, I pressed my ear against the wall, but it was hard to make out what the panic-riddled voices were screaming over what sounded like an exorcism. *What the hell is going-* **CRASH!** Something was flung into the other side of the wall mere inches from my face, causing dust to scatter when it quaked.

As I staggered backwards, Doctor Hailey scrambled off the desk when something was launched into the door, making it audibly crack. A woman's harrowing cry then ripped through the carnage, and a deep, enrooted need to help overpowered my senses. *I can't just stand here and do nothing!*

Lunging for the desk, I was unexpectedly pulled back by Doctor Hailey, who shook his head once.
"Why?!" I mouthed, shrugging off his hold.
He clearly couldn't lipread as his brow furrowed; a baffled look now graced his hatchet face.

The screaming then intensified, and I knew she would die if I didn't step in. *I've got to do something!*
Grasping the desk to slide it away, Doctor Hailey swiftly snatched the other end, firmly holding it in place.
"What are you doing?!" I barked over the ruckus, luckily drowned out by another insufferable cry and bloodcurdling groan.
With another shake of his head, Doctor Hailey furiously mouthed, "Don-"

SMASH! The door splintered and cracked when something heavy was thrown into it again. The fractured wood zigzagged down, threatening to burst open at any moment. I immediately froze, frightened it would shatter and the perpetrator would see us all standing there like lambs to slaughter.

A terrified gasp was the last thing I heard before something long and sharp perforated through the door, causing us all to jump back in alarm. *Is that a fucking knife?!* I noted the blade was smeared red. It was then yanked back through the door; a thud swiftly followed.

I couldn't help but stare wide-eyed at Doctor Hailey, my mouth agape as it dawned on me- *We've got to go out there if we want to get to the maintenance room...*

Footsteps then disappeared in the direction of Doctor Sasin's office; I prayed it was the perpetrator leaving, no longer searching for us.

"Hopefully, he thinks we've gone to the female ward..." Doctor Hailey muttered, carefully sliding the desk away, "So we need to leave now before he comes back."

"**Now?!**" I gaped, "But he's literally just left!"

"And he would've been dead if you had pulled the trigger..." He bitterly retorted, anger blazing behind his dark, penetrating eyes as he unlocked the door.

But I don't know how to use it! I exclaimed in frustration, staring down at the gun in question still in my sweaty grasp.

Shifting his attention to Jack and Adi, Doctor Hailey instructed, "You two stay here."

"Like sitting fucking ducks?!" Jack growled, defiantly shaking her head, "I don't think so! We're coming with you!"

"Are we?!" Adi countered, stunned.

"No, you're not!" Doctor Hailey rumbled, unexpectedly snatching me up by the front of my shirt.

I was momentarily taken aback until I realised he was retrieving the camera.

"I trust you two to take the evidence to the police if we're not back." Doctor Hailey continued before speaking directly to Jack, "Keep this safe."

He passed the camera to her, and she stared suspiciously down at it.

"What if I don't?" She wondered, peering up at him almost threateningly.

"Then you'll be allowing this to happen to other innocent people..." Doctor Hailey retorted, and that comment alone made Jack tuck the camera safely away down the front of her shirt.

"If we're not back in an hour, I want you both to go straight to the church." Doctor Hailey advised, fumbling with his keys, "You'll find the vestry room towards the back. Go in there, and you'll see a bookcase with a trunk in front of it. Move them both, and you'll find the door that this key belongs to." He then produced an old, rusty-looking key that he handed to Jack.

"But what if we can't get through?" Adi piped up, "What if the church is barricaded?"

Please don't tell me that's the only way outta here... I murmured, a sinking feeling growing in the pit of my stomach.

"There's a way out through the nurses' block, or even through the boiler house and into the drying grounds." Doctor Hailey responded, filling me with relief, "But I can almost guarantee those areas will be locked down as well." And all hope was swiftly dashed away.

"Stay hidden until we get back." He cautioned, "As long as everything goes smoothly, we shouldn't be too long."

His gaze shifted to me before he nodded for us to leave. *I guess I've got no choice in the matter...* I uttered, pressing my lips together as he opened the door, which groaned in protest.

"You first." Doctor Hailey offered, beckoning with a sweep of his hand for me to step out into the corridor.

Anxiously rubbing my right hand around the back of my neck, I reluctantly stepped outside.

I was so concerned with checking both ways that I tripped up on something slumped in front of the door. *Whoa!* Slamming my hands against the opposite window, I barely caught myself.

"Careful." Doctor Hailey advised as I turned around, my eyes following his and locking onto the body I had accidentally stumbled over.

Holy shit! An uncontrollable shudder swept throughout me, my eyes unable to close as I took in the oozing, gaping lacerations that had drenched the once-blue dress. *That... That... That **can't** be a body!* Slowly shaking my head in denial, I then regretfully saw the misshapen limbs. They were so loose and floppy, I couldn't believe they were once held together with bones.

How... But... Why- How?! My thoughts were fragmented when I glanced over chunks of bloodstained, blonde hair that lay in matted clumps beside the corpse, looking like something a cat had thrown up. But what caused the burn of bile in the back of my throat was when I saw what remained of the face; it was perfectly carved in two. Blood seeped from the cavernous wound, exposing bone, teeth, muscle, and even brain matter. *Oh God, fuck! There's so much blood!*

Gripping my throat, I was finally able to retreat and put some much-needed distance between myself and the body. *Who the fuck could do something like this?!* Screwing my face up in disgust, I averted my gaze to Doctor Hailey, who looked completely unfazed.

"If you're about done, we need to hurry." He said, not waiting for me to reply before darting toward the stairwell.

It was only then I spotted two more decapitated bodies further down. *Jesus!* I gaped, grimacing when I passed what was left of them, only to notice their once-white uniforms had been ripped to shreds. Their thick, beefy arms appeared to have been torn from their sockets. *How the hell was someone able to take on a nurse **and** two orderlies?!*

"Hurry up!" Doctor Hailey abruptly hawked, my attention snapping to him by the stairwell door, "We haven't got time to dilly-dally!"

He's right. The guy who did this could be back at any moment. That thought alone sent a shiver up my spine, so I rushed over, and he ripped open the door. Our shoes pounded against the steps, but they were quickly drowned out by the siren as well as the bloodcurdling screams still ricocheting throughout the asylum.

Once we reached the bottom, Doctor Hailey said, "The maintenance room is near solitary confinement, so we'll head straight down the corridor when I open this door."

I knew that hallway well; it was where all the therapy rooms were.

When I nodded, he continued, "We'll carry on down the long corridor that leads to solitary confinement, but we'll turn left at the intersection before we reach it. The maintenance room is at the very end of that corridor."

Just as Doctor Hailey opened the door a fraction, he sharply commented, "Make sure you pull the trigger this time..." And he gestured down at the gun with a nod.

BUT I DON'T KNOW HOW TO USE IT! I inwardly screamed, having to clear my throat to stop my volatile nature from rearing its ugly head.

I knew the mechanics of a gun, but the actual thought of pulling a trigger went against the very grain of my being. *I need to say something before I put both our lives at risk.*

"Look," I earnestly began before he could fully open the door, "I don't know how to use this."

Bringing the gun up in question, his dark, penetrating eyes locked onto it. There was no denying his disbelief when he turned away, briefly covering his mouth with his hand before finally looking back up at me.

"You don't know how to use a gun?!" Doctor Hailey yelled, his face reddening as anger consumed him.

Unable to reply, I merely wetted my lips and nodded.

"Then why the fuck did you assure me you were the man for this job?! That you're qualified up to the fucking eyeballs and had extensive training?!" He demanded, his voice deepening into a threatening undertone.

Again, I couldn't speak. I couldn't even look at him. *What do I say? That I'm not who he thinks I am?*

"I knew something was off with you..." He uttered with a shake of his head.

"Look," I tried to reason with him, but he suddenly snatched the gun out of my sweaty grasp, stunning me into silence.

Wait, what's he doing?! My thoughts immediately shifted to the worst-case scenario. *Is he gonna shoot me?!* Much to my surprise, Doctor Hailey merely checked the chamber, and I saw six bullets. He then passed the gun back once he had clicked it into place. *Erm... What just happened?...* Confused, I stared at him with a furrowed brow.

"The safety's off," He commented, "So don't pull the trigger until you're- Oh, what am I thinking? You probably don't even know what the trigger is." And he pointed at it.

I wasn't sure if he was trying to be funny or genuinely thought I had no idea what the trigger was.

"Yeah, I know." I bluntly responded, which only seemed to shock him.

"You do? You actually know something?" He rhetorically asked, and it was right then that I realised he was being condescending.

Breathe, just breathe.

Without another word, Doctor Hailey yanked open the door, and the ear-piercing screams shattered the tension between us. The lights were still ablaze with a threatening red, matching the gore dashed across the floorboards and up the walls, as if someone had left a sprinkler on.

Following him out into the corridor, I peered right and saw the gated entrance to the male ward hanging off its hinges. A female patient was on the other side, hovering by the wall. *What the hell's she doing?!* I gawked, staring between her and what appeared to be an Ouija board drawn in blood on the wall. *That's... That's not her blood, is it?...* Judging by the oozing, makeshift paint brush that was once her index finger, I realised it was. *But why?! Why would you do that to yourself?!*

Then I noted she had done a lot worse. My body turned cold when I saw she was using her eyeball as a planchette, rolling it between the yes and no. Pressing the back of my hand against my nose when she turned to look at me with her one good eye, I immediately glanced away, noticing Doctor Hailey was already halfway down the corridor.

Retreating after him, the late afternoon sun bathed my face as it seeped in through the barred windows, which were smeared with bloody handprints and other bodily fluids. *This place seriously went to shit fast...* When I finally caught up to Doctor Hailey, who was waiting for me at the end of the hallway, we headed down the long straight leading to solitary confinement. The red lights intensified as there were no windows, masking the gore-riddled walls and floor.

Then I could hear something. **THUD!** *What's that?* **THUD!** The noise was coming from somewhere just up ahead. Glancing quizzically at Doctor Hailey, he looked just as puzzled. He then immediately slowed, as did I, and we crept down the hall until we saw a male patient clad in a straightjacket. *What's he doing?...* He stood by the intersection, repeatedly banging his face against the wall, leaving a patch of blood in his wake. Cringing at the sight, I quickly peered down at Doctor Hailey to see his reaction, but he was just as unfazed by this as he had been with everything else. *It's like he doesn't care...*

"Come on." He quietly muttered to me, giving the patient a wide berth and heading left.
I silently followed, not once taking my eyes off the inmate,

fearing he would turn his attention upon us. *Not that he can do much…*

We then rushed down the new corridor once we were a safe enough distance away, passing a handful of doors only on our left. It wasn't until we reached the very end, where the hallway veered off right, that we stopped at the last entry. *This is it!* I breathed when I saw **MAINTENANCE** on the plaque. Once Doctor Hailey had unlocked it, he ushered me into the small, dimly lit room that was barely big enough to swing a cat.

Hacksaw. Hacksaw. Where would a hacksaw be? I mulled as he closed the door; all the while, I stared around at the racks along the walls on either side. *There must be one in here!*

"Keep your eyes open for a hacksaw." I instructed, tucking the gun into the back of my trousers whilst I searched.

"Hacksaw aside," Doctor Hailey sceptically began, inspecting a drill piece as he said, "Why did you lie to me?"

Lie to him? I was taken aback by his question. *Is he going on about the gun?*

"I didn't-"

"Thinking about it, why did you say you're the man for the job when you aren't?" He interjected, discarding the drill piece with a clatter.

Of all times, what's with the questions now?

I stopped searching and answered with clenched teeth, "I don't know…"

"Was it meant to be some elaborate joke that went too far, and you couldn't back out?!" Doctor Hailey heatedly tacked on, his eyes cold and flinty as he stared at me.

Is he trying to piss me off? Ignoring him, I continued my hunt for the hacksaw. **BANG!** But my silence clearly rubbed him the wrong way as he pounded a fist against one of the racks.

"Was it to prove some kind of point to your peers who, perhaps, have more balls than you'll ever have?!" Doctor Hailey furiously declared, evidently wanting some kind of reaction.

"I don't know!" I replied a little too readily, refusing to look at him.

Unexpectedly, he laughed at my response, gaining my attention once more. *I'm seriously gonna lose my shit with him in a minute!* I fumed, staring at him through narrowed eyes as he now inspected a crowbar.

"No... You don't know anything, do you?" He criticised me, and I couldn't deal with his opinionated behaviour a moment longer. I had no restraint over my actions when I shoved him hard against the door; my lips pulled back into a snarl as I gutturally roared, "I DON'T KNOW, OKAY?! **I DON'T FUCKING REMEMBER ANYTHING!**"

DING! The crowbar slipped from Doctor Hailey's grasp, a realisation engulfing him. My rage instantly subsided, replaced by apprehension. *Why's he looking at me like that?* As I pulled away, I felt a tightness form in my chest the longer he stared at me.

After a moment of silence, Doctor Hailey repeated, "You don't remember '**anything**'?" But he didn't allow me to reply before muttering to himself, "That makes so much sense... Whatever Fred did to him has made him forget everything, not just where the camera was..."

Now it was my turn for the realisation to set in. *He thinks the therapy sessions have given me memory loss...* I wasn't going to correct him; it gave me some much-needed relief from the tension growing in the atmosphere.

"Have you found a hacksaw yet?" I asked, changing the subject, which snapped him back to reality.

Plucking up the crowbar with a shake of his head, Doctor Hailey wondered, "No, but will this work to bend the bars?"

Well, it'll probably bend them at the wrong angle, but it's better than nothing.

"Yeah," I nodded, "It'll bend them."

"Good!" He delightedly exclaimed, tucking the crowbar under his arm, "Then let's head back."

Doctor Hailey then opened the door only to freeze when he came face to face with the barrel of a gun. At first, there was no denying the fear that consumed me, but it swiftly dissipated when I saw who was holding it. *He's not gonna shoot us, is he?* Staring hard at Doctor Kröger, I tried to figure out if he was capable of pulling a trigger. *No, he's not gonna do anything.* His knees were knocking, and the gun was trembling in his grasp.

Doctor Hailey must have also seen the apprehension plastered upon Doctor Kröger's sweaty face as he urged, "Step aside, Erik."

Shaking his head, Doctor Kröger stammered, "I-I'm suh-sorry, Elon."

"'**Sorry**'?" He repeated with a furrowed brow, "Why are you saying sorry?"

"Buh-Because... Because if Mr Moon doesn't come viz me," Doctor Kröger tremulously explained, swallowing hard, "Zee patient you've shtowed in mein office von't be alive fur much longer."

Wait, how does he know we were in his office?!

"Hand over Mr Moon," Doctor Kröger carried on, wiping away the sweat on his brow with a forearm, "Ozervise, I vill schoot you."

"No, you won't." Doctor Hailey stated matter-of-factly, unimpressed.

He then slapped the crowbar against the palm of his hand, threatening, "So move aside, Erik, before I **make** you."

He took an intimidating step forward, but Doctor Kröger didn't budge.

Only then did I notice the quiet, underlying urgency about Doctor Kröger, something I couldn't quite put my finger on. *Would he really shoot him?* My gaze momentarily shifted to Doctor Hailey while reaching for the holstered gun with my left hand, slowly grasping the grip and resting my index finger against the trigger.

Taking a shaky step back, Doctor Kröger adamantly declared, "I **vill**! I vill schoot you! I vill-"

With lightning-quick reflexes, Doctor Hailey dropped the crowbar and lunged for the gun, but Doctor Kröger had an iron-like grip.

"LET! GO!" Doctor Hailey spat through gritted teeth, trying to yank the hardware free with both hands, causing Doctor Kröger to stagger forward.

"**NEIN!**" He shrieked, his hold never wavering.

I knew I needed to step in as Doctor Hailey was my only way out of this hellhole. *And I'll be damned if this German prick fucking kills him!* Instinctively, I brought the gun round in front of me, fully extending it toward Doctor Kröger with straight arms locked in place.

"PUT THE GUN DOWN NOW!" I implored, but no one listened; they hadn't even noticed the hardware, never mind the click of the hammer when I pulled it back.

"He promised he'd let me go if I did as he zaid!" Doctor Kröger desperately explained, as if that would change the entire situation.

"I don't care what **he** promised!" Doctor Hailey growled. He then wrenched the German doctor closer, the gun now clutched to his chest.

"I SAID PUT THE GUN DOWN!" I commanded, yet was ignored again.

"You're not taking him anywhere!" Doctor Hailey continued, twisting his body in an attempt to force Doctor Kröger to let go of the weapon.

Readying myself to fire a warning shot, I firmly planted my feet shoulder-width apart and gutturally roared, "**DROP THE FUCKING GUN!**"

BANG! For a moment, while the ear-piercing sound ricocheted around the small maintenance room, I thought I had pulled the trigger until I realised the hammer was still pulled back on my gun.

Abruptly, the two doctors parted, and blood hit the floor with a pitter-patter. *Holy shit!* I had no idea who was bleeding until Doctor Hailey stared at his trembling, gore-riddled hands that were pressed against his stomach, blood now oozing through his white coat like ink seeping into a piece of parchment. *No, no, no, this isn't happening!*

Doctor Hailey staggered backwards into the wall with a thud, and I was about to rush over when the click of a hammer stilled me in my tracks.

"Drop zee gun." Doctor Kröger adjured, my gaze shifting to him, his weapon pointing at me.

This... This can't be happening! This seriously can't be happening!

As I stared down the barrel of the gun, all I could think of was my family and how I couldn't bear the thought of leaving my children without a father. *I **can't** do that to them!* I almost did as Doctor Kröger said until the rational part of my mind remembered something. ***'Hand over Mr Moon.'*** His words cleared my doubt. *He needs me, or at least someone else does.* I knew then he had no intention of killing me.

"I zaid '**Drop zee gun**.'." Doctor Kröger sternly reiterated.

A playful grin pulled at the corner of my lips when I countered, "Or what? You'll shoot me?"

An awareness then suddenly encompassed him, as if it had only just dawned on him that his gun was useless against me.

After a moment of silence, Doctor Kröger regretfully agreed, "Nein... I von't schoot you..."
His blue eyes shifted to Doctor Hailey leaning precariously against the tool rack.
"But he vill die along viz your friend in mein office." He added, a slow, malicious smile spreading across his face, "Unless you come viz me."

But what's to stop him from killing them, anyway? That was the question that had me falter. I needed reassurance that no one would get hurt.

"How can I trust you?" I interrogated, my eyes narrowing as I searched Doctor Kröger's face for any tell-tale signs that he was lying.
"How can I be sure they won't get hurt? That he won't die?" I then briefly glanced at Doctor Hailey, who was paling by the second.

Unsurprisingly, Doctor Kröger didn't say anything. I could tell he was nervous by the slight wobble of his Adam's apple whenever he swallowed hard. *He has no intention of keeping his word...* I realised when his blue eyes flitted between my gun and my gaze, his hand repeatedly clenching by his side in anticipation.

"Don't be so stupid, Rick!" Doctor Hailey piped up, distracting me, "You can't trust-"
THUMP! Doctor Kröger unexpectedly charged into me while reaching for the gun with his right hand. **OOF!** The wind was knocked out of me, and our combined weight toppled us off balance. My grip on the weapon automatically tightened as I held onto it for dear life, unintentionally squeezing the trigger.
BANG! The kickback had me stagger into the tool rack with a thud; a harrowing scream sliced through the whip-like sound the bullet had left in its wake.

"**MEIN HAND! MEIN HAND!**" Doctor Kröger screeched, and that was when I saw the ragged mess left behind from the bullet.
"**MEIN HAND!**" He continued to cry, clutching the gaping, gushing wound close to his chest, soaking his white coat crimson.
Did... Did I do that?... Shaking my head in denial, I glimpsed down at the gun still in my grasp; smoke rose from the barrel.

"We need to leave!" Doctor Hailey urged, gingerly snatching up the gun Doctor Kröger must have dropped. "Someone would've heard them go off!" He added, using the rack to help guide him to the door.

Shit, he's right! Hastily picking up the crowbar, I went to follow him but was yanked to a halt.

"**PLEASE!**" Doctor Kröger begged, grasping my bicep, "Help me!" But I didn't know how; after all, he was the doctor, not I.

I didn't get the chance to reply before Doctor Hailey pointed his gun at the German doctor, who stared at him like a deer caught in the headlights.

"Let him go, Erik." Doctor Hailey calmly but coldly prompted, pulling back the hammer.

Doctor Kröger reluctantly released me but still tried to leave; however, Doctor Hailey slapped a hand down in the doorway once I was out, blocking the way.

"Vait, you're leaving me here?!" The German doctor panicked, and Doctor Hailey sighed a half-arsed apology, "I'm sorry, Erik, but I don't like you. So, I hope for your sake that you bleed out quickly."

With a pained groan, Doctor Hailey shoved him back inside and locked the door.

"LET ME OUT!" Doctor Kröger shrieked while pounding on the door, "PLEASE!" **BANG!** "LET ME OUT!" **BANG!**

"Come on! We need to get out of here!" Doctor Hailey pressed, and as if on cue, footsteps resounded along the corridor directly ahead.

I could see he was struggling to stand, so I supported him as we rushed back the way we came. To my relief, the only person we passed was the inmate banging his face against the wall; even the patient who had painted an Ouija board was nowhere to be seen.

We then reached the top of the stairwell, bypassed the dead bodies, and finally made it back to Doctor Kröger's office. *I don't know if we'll make it outta here in time. I really need to get him to a hospital.* I peered down worriedly at Doctor Hailey, who was struggling to stay conscious. *Hopefully, there are some bandages in here to patch him up with.*

Shunting the door open, I hurried inside.

"I need one of you..." I began, but my voice trailed off when I clocked Randy staring gleefully at us.

He sat on one of the leather chairs he had moved into the middle of the room. *What the fuck's he doing here?!* That thought was short-lived when I saw Adi knelt in between his legs facing us, a shard of glass pressed against his throat.

"Well, don't just stand there!" Randy eagerly proclaimed, gesturing for us to step further inside with his free hand, "Come in and close the door behind ya."

A wicked smile grew on his gaunt face, revealing his rotten and cracked teeth, "We've got some talkin' ter do."

Chapter Ten

Times up!

"Don't make me 'ave ter ask again." Randy growled when neither Doctor Hailey nor I budged an inch, but I did as he said this time.

I carefully guided Doctor Hailey to the leather sofa, wondering, "What do you want, Randy?" I then glanced over my shoulder at him.

"Awh, that's simple!" He proclaimed excitedly, not continuing until I set Doctor Hailey down and gave him my full, undivided attention, "My favour."

'If I do this for ya, then ya owe me a favour.'

Randy's voice infiltrated my mind, chilling me to the very core. *But I already did his favour...* I remembered. *He wanted to stay when I spoke to Jack...*

Clasping my hands together, I turned to Randy, reminding him, "You already had your favour when you wanted to stay in Jack's cell."

"Yer gonna argue with someone holdin' glass ter yer pal's throat?" He countered, jabbing the shard into Adi's neck, who squealed in fright.

"So back ter my favour." He eagerly continued, "Ya see, Adi **kindly** explained why 'e's runnin' 'round with a cop and doctor."

Wait, he told him?! Shocked, I peered at Adi, who couldn't look at me, clearly ashamed for telling Randy everything.

"Yer plannin' an escape, and I want ter be part of that plan." Randy grinned maniacally at me, "What ya say?"

"No." Doctor Hailey bluntly intervened, taking me aback. *What's he doing?!* I fretted, repeatedly rubbing my face as I watched the heated scenario unravel before me.

"'**No**'?" Randy echoed as he rose to his feet, his cunning blue eyes snapping over to Doctor Hailey, "What ya mean no?"

He then hoisted Adi up by the scruff of his hair, pressing the shard of glass harder against his throat, making him cry out in pain. *No, this isn't happening! I'm **not** gonna stand here and let him kill Adi!*

Rounding on Doctor Hailey, I demanded, "Yeah, what do you mean '**no**'?" And I panickily gestured over to Adi, "He'll kill him if we don't!"

"Could you live with a clear conscience knowing you willingly let a killer free?" Doctor Hailey coldly retorted.

He tried to sit up, but a pained groan leaked from his lips, a reminder that he was living on borrowed time.

"Or could ya live with yerself knowin' ya let a pal die?" Randy retaliated, jamming the shard a little harder into Adi's throat, now making him bleed.

Stunned, a knot formed in my stomach. *They can't expect me to make this decision!*

"Come on, tick tock, tick tock." Randy goaded while Doctor Hailey just stared at me with eyes like daggers.

*There must be a way I can save Adi **and** get rid of Randy.* But my mind was drawing a blank.

"Tick tock, tick tock." Randy relentlessly chanted over and over, distracting me from finding an alternative solution.

I just need him to shut up for a minute!

"Times tickin', Trav." He persisted, his blue eyes lighting up mockingly, "What's it goin' ter be? Tick tock, tick tock."

I immediately glanced at Doctor Hailey, who merely shook his head. *Is he seriously not gonna help-*

"**DING, DING, DING!**" Randy suddenly hollered, "Times up!"

He dug the shard deeper into Adi's throat, causing blood to drip down his neck.

In a desperate attempt to save Adi's life, I beseeched, "Okay, okay, wait!" And I raised my hands that were still holding the crowbar and gun in a stop gesture, "We'll take you; just drop the glass!"

"Pfft!" Randy unexpectedly scoffed, "What do ya take me for? Some kinda mug?" He gestured between my weapons with the shard, "I ain't droppin' a thing until ya drop those. Ya get?"

"Don't you dare!" Doctor Hailey warned when I started to lower them, "You can't trust him! He'll just kill Adi, anyway!"

"And fuck my chances of gettin' outta 'ere?" Randy rhetorically asked with a raised brow, his eyes flitting back to me as he ordered, "Put them down." And I did as he asked.

"Now," He carried on, pressing the shard back to Adi's throat, "Kick the gun over 'ere and tell me 'ow we're gettin' outta 'ere."

"Rick, don't you fucking think about giving him that gun!" Doctor Hailey snapped, fiercely trying to stand but not having the strength.

A wicked laugh echoed from Randy, gaining my attention just as he taunted, "What's it gonna be, Trav?" And he dug the glass even deeper into Adi's neck, "Ya gonna give me the gun? Or ya gonna let yer pal die?"

It felt like Doctor Hailey and Randy were the Angel and Devil sitting on my shoulders, but I couldn't tell which they were. *Fuck this entire situation!*

Not daring to glimpse at Doctor Hailey in fear of his reaction, I decidedly kicked the gun over to Randy, who smiled gleefully at me.

"I'm glad ter see ya made the right choice." He chuckled, half-bending down to scoop up the gun before discarding the glass with a smash.

"Now," Randy continued, pressing the gun to Adi's head, "'ow we gettin' outta 'ere?"

A tightness formed in my chest as I glanced uneasily at the window.

"That way." I reluctantly replied, peering back over at Randy.

Confused, he stared between me and the window for a heartbeat.

"'ow? It's barred." He wondered, and Doctor Hailey bitterly said, "If you're so Goddamn clever, why don't you figure it out yourself?..." There was no denying that comment irritated Randy by the slight twitch underneath his bulbous left eye, but he said nothing.

After what felt like a lifetime of Randy trying to work out how we had intended to escape through the window, his eyes eventually landed on the crowbar, lighting up in realisation.

"Ya plan ter bend the bars, right?" He eagerly asked, carrying on once I nodded, "Then what the fuck yer waitin' for?! **Do it!**" *What's gonna happen after I've bent them?...* I fretted, hesitantly snatching up the crowbar.

"Now 'urry up!" He growled, waving his gun towards the window.

Unable to stop glowering at Randy with cold, flinty eyes, my blood boiled at the notion that this man had all the control he needed to get what he wanted. *I'll be fucking damned if he gets outta here!* But right now, there was very little I could do, so I hooked the crowbar around one of the middle bars and tried my hardest to bend it. It was exhausting, but the bars slowly started to bow.

I just need that gun, then I'll be the one in control... I deliberated, glimpsing at Adi trembling against the hardware still pressed to his head. *But how am I gonna get it?* I then circled my gaze over to Doctor Hailey still slumped on the sofa, his chest rising and falling with every ragged breath he took. *I need to get him outta here and to a hospital.* But my inner pessimist didn't think he would make it.

Once I bent the last bar, I swiped the sweat off my brow with the back of my hand.

"It's done." I disclosed, turning to Randy, "All we've got to do is open or smash the window, and then we can get out of here." *If he goes first, I can crack this over his head.* I deviously mulled, clutching the crowbar a little tighter.

"It's done?" Randy repeated, unconvinced.

His cunning blue eyes then peered over at my handiwork when I nodded, and a sadistic smile slowly spread across his gaunt face. "Excellent!" He purred in delight, his attention then shifting back down to Adi.

BANG! The whip-like sound of a bullet ricocheted throughout the office before Adi's body slumped to the floor with a thud. **BANG!** Another swiftly followed, and a gut-wrenching moan echoed from Doctor Hailey, who rolled off the sofa and disappeared from view.

Silence soon deafened the room. It wasn't until the fresh stench of gore wafted up my nose, along with the pungent smell of gunfire, that the whole ordeal finally sunk in, and I realised what Randy did.

Pressing a fist to my mouth, my voice warbled, "You... You fuh-fucking killed them!"
Smirking like the vile murderer he was, Randy pointed the gun at me, "Ya should've listened to yer doctor pal."
It was at that moment I saw red. *I'll fucking kill him!* An indescribable sensation of raw, unchecked strength consumed me. A rush of adrenaline then swept throughout my body. Now grasping the crowbar with both hands, I was unable to ignore the need – the want - to hurt him. *I'll kill him for what he fucking did!*

Before Randy could pull the trigger, I lunged for him, swinging the sturdy metal across his torso as well as his hands. **BANG!** The gun went off before he dropped it with a cry. I had no idea if he had managed to shoot me; I was too pumped with rage to notice anything but him amidst my red haze. I couldn't even hear him beg as a pounding now echoed in my ears.

Bringing the crowbar back up, a guttural roar escaped my hold when I smacked it against Randy's face. His nose split open like a Chestburster emerging from its host in Alien, causing blood to gush like Niagara Falls. Collapsing to the floor like the sack of shit he was, Randy scurried backwards on his arse while holding up a hand, a silent gesture for me to stop. I had no intention of stopping. Now he had nowhere else to go since his back was flush against a filing cabinet; I slowly advanced on him.

"PLEASE!" Randy desperately beseeched through the gore dripping down his face, "If ya let me go, I can get ya whatever ya want once we're outta 'ere!" But I was not interested in bargaining with him.
"Anything ya want!" He pitifully carried on, staring up and up when I came to tower over him, "I swear, anything ya want!"
His pathetic act had me ruthlessly wondering, "And what did you say to all your victims when they were begging for their lives?"
A realisation then abruptly dawned on him now the tables had turned.

Mercilessly, I swung the crowbar down, striking Randy right between the eyes and ripping his flesh open. I could see he was still alive by the pain shimmering behind his once cunning blue eyes, but he was motionless like a ragdoll. It was then I should have stopped. He would not get up anytime soon, and I had made my point by putting him in his place. But I didn't stop.

With the hooked end pointing downwards, I smashed it against Randy's face. **CRACK!** Chunks of skin just beneath his left eye were gouged out. **SMACK!** The next blow made his eyeball pop out of its socket, now hanging down his cheek by a bloody thread. **CRUNCH!** The split beak of the crowbar shattered through the top of Randy's skull, ripping out a wrinkled, lumpy mass of flesh that hit the floor with an audible squelch.

"**I SAID STOP!**" A voice barked as I was about to bring the crowbar back down.

Suddenly, a hand lunged for it mid-swing, snapping me back to my senses. The first thing I saw were dark, penetrating eyes staring intently into mine. *He... He's not dead?!* I couldn't see another bullet wound. *Did Randy miss?*

"Let! Go! Of the! Crowbar!" Doctor Hailey exhorted through gritted teeth, struggling against the tension of my weight still trying to bring the metal bar down.

Only then did I become aware of it in my grasp. *What the?!* It was the warm blood dripping down my hands that I noticed first, rhythmically hitting the floor with a pitter-patter. Then I clocked Randy, or at least what was left of him. I wouldn't have recognised him if I had just walked into the room as his face was completely caved in.

What the fuck did I do?! Abruptly releasing the crowbar, I stared unblinking at Randy before the reality that I was a murderer crashed over me like a tsunami. Revulsion hit me out of nowhere, along with the stench of gore that hung in the atmosphere. Unable to keep the vomit at bay, I threw up all over the hardwood floor.

"When you're about done, we need to leave." Doctor Hailey said, dropping the crowbar with a ding.

Bringing a fist to my moist lips, I swallowed a lump of bile before peering over at him. He had just finished wiping his bloodstained hands down his trouser legs before stiffly kneeling beside Adi's motionless body, pressing two fingers to his neck.

Is he still alive?! I waited with bated breath for Doctor Hailey to give the good news; however, he merely lowered his hand, not uttering a word. Grief and regret instantly consumed every fibre of my being. *He's dead... Dead because of me...* Averting my gaze, I couldn't stop the hitch in the back of my throat. *Doctor Hailey was right; I should **never** have given Randy that gun!* But I would be damned if I lost anyone else.

Lowering my hand, I echoed Doctor Hailey's words, "We need to leave!"

A small smile lifted the corner of his mouth, "It's about time you started talking sense."

While Doctor Hailey shakily rose to his feet, I grabbed the gun Randy had dropped, instinctively checking the chamber and counting two bullets. I then swiftly diverted my attention, refusing to look at his body so I could put that horrid image to the very back of my mind, but even just thinking about what I did made me want to be sick. *I need to get the hell outta here!*

Turning back to Doctor Hailey, I realised he was anxiously staring around. *What's he doing?*

His eyes locked onto mine, and he worriedly asked, "Where's Jack?"

Where's Jack? I repeated, confused at first, certain I had misheard him. But it soon became apparent she was not in the office. *Then where the hell is she?!*

"Wasn't she in here when we got back?" I wondered, and Doctor Hailey shook his head, his words barely audible as he groaned, "I don't recall seeing her."

"Then where the hell's she gone?!"

Wracking my brain, I tried to figure out why she had left and when. *Didn't he tell her to stay here?* I thought back over the conversation before Doctor Hailey and I searched for a hacksaw. ***'You two stay here.'*** His instructions infiltrated my mind before he gave Jack my hidden camera. ***'If we're not back in an hour, I want you both to go straight to the church.'*** *Maybe that's where she's gone...*

Heading for the door, I said, "I'm gonna find her." But Doctor Hailey's comment stopped me, "Do you know exactly how big this hospital is? It'll be like trying to find a needle in a haystack."

"Maybe," I agreed, turning to see him resting against the chair, "But my bet is she's gone to the church."

Staring at me with narrowed eyes, he croakily pondered, "Do you even know where the church is?"

I thought he was being condescending until I saw the concern shimmering behind his dark eyes.

Nodding, I replied, "It's by the entrance."

"Very well..." Doctor Hailey uttered, scrubbing a hand across his pale, sweaty face, "Then I must warn you of Zed Stoltzfus."
I couldn't help but blink in confusion, "Zed who?"
"Stoltzfus." He said again, lowering his hand to pinch the skin at his throat.
It didn't matter how many times he repeated the name; I still had no clue who this person was.
"Again, who?" I pressed, but Doctor Hailey grew unusually quiet and just stared at the splintered door.
When he didn't reply, I heatedly urged, "**Who?!**"
His attention never drifted from the door when he finally responded, "The patient who did that."
"**Them?!**" I hawked, remembering what he did to those bodies out in the hallway before his deep, otherworldly voice invaded my mind.
'Doctoooooor Haaaaaaaileeeeeeey...'
Looking back at Doctor Hailey, I anxiously asked, "Why do I need to worry about him?"
"Because he and everyone else in this hospital now know who you are and that we're working together." He explained in a strained tone, wetting his lips before continuing, "If Zed manages to get his hands on you, I dread to think what he'll do to you just to get to me."
But why's Zed after him?
A need to know – to understand – what was going on piqued my interest, so I curiously pried, "And why does he want you?"
Waving a hand dismissively, Doctor Hailey replied, "We don't have the time for-"
"Don't tell me to be careful of some nutjob and then not tell me why he's after you!" I sharply interrupted, my pulse quickening in irritation when I noted he was just as equally annoyed by the audible grinding of his teeth.
After a while of us just staring at one another with narrowed eyes, Doctor Hailey reluctantly clarified, "To cut a long story short, I'm the one who got him admitted here." And I was now only consumed by more questions.
"Wait, what, how?!" I blabbered, shocked, "What did he do?"
"Look," He began, holding up a shaky hand, "We don't have time-"

"**JUST FUCKING ANSWER ME!**" I volatilely snapped, taking him aback.

After a brief moment of silence, Doctor Hailey peered at me with a fixed look of concentration.

"I first met Zed when I worked at Blackwater Mental Asylum, where he was also a psychiatric doctor." He admitted, stunning me.

Wait, he was a doctor?! I gaped, horrified. *What did he do to end up as a patient?!*

"He was honestly the kindest, friendliest person I had ever met," He unwillingly carried on, "But that's obviously what they all want you to think."

"For months, no one looked into why his patients were dying. Whenever Zed was questioned, he always had a plausible explanation. '**Well, he was in his eighties...**'. '**You are aware he tried to hang himself multiple times before now, right?**'. '**That's what happens when the orderlies don't pat them down, they sneak things into their cells they shouldn't...**'. Honestly, I'm ashamed of myself for not seeing beyond his bullshit excuses, but no one else did either."

"The next thing everyone overlooked was the bodies. No one ever saw them after Zed announced the patient's death, which usually happened shortly after his sessions. I think it was probably..." Doctor Hailey trailed off, counting on his fingers, "The eighth, tenth time I had to explain to the patient's family we no longer had the body that I realised something wasn't quite right."

What... What was he doing with them?... I apprehensively wondered, not sure if I actually wanted to know.

"When I found out what Zed was doing, I gathered enough evidence and went straight to the police." Doctor Hailey said, his voice strained, "But even after he was arrested, I couldn't bring myself to continue working at Blackwater Mental Asylum. That was when I thought my stars had aligned, as I was offered the job of head doctor here." He then gestured around at Merriwell Sanatorium with a self-deprecated laugh, "Funny thing is, after Zed was found not guilty by reason of insanity, he was placed here under my care..."

As interesting as that was, it still didn't answer my question. What is this Zed guy capable of?

"What did he do to them exactly?" I pressed, causing a grim look to wash over Doctor Hailey's pale face.

He wasn't someone easily fazed, so I began to worry. *What the hell will he do if he gets his hands on me?!* I fretted, inhaling a few steady breaths in an attempt to calm my inner turmoil.

"That doesn't matter." Doctor Hailey stated, the disgust on his face long gone, "All you need to know is he's a very dangerous man, so avoid him at all costs."

He then instantly turned away and tentatively made his way over to the sofa, ending the conversation before I could question him further. *Is he even gonna be alive when I get back?* I deliberated when he slumped down onto it with an audible groan.

Shooting Doctor Hailey one last glance, I hesitantly left the safe confines of the office. To my relief, the upper level appeared empty; the only commotion could be heard from somewhere down below. *But that doesn't mean someone isn't lurking nearby...* That thought alone sent a shiver up my spine. *I just want to get outta here!* Shaking off my unease, I made a dash for the stairwell, relieved no one emerged from any of the offices.

Keeping my gun poised, I descended the stairs and opened the door. The horrific pandemonium crashed over me like a tidal wave, dousing me with an indescribable fear. *I don't like this!* I couldn't pinpoint exactly where the noise was coming from; it swarmed me from every angle. *I don't fucking like this!* Struggling to still my shaky limbs, I focused on my one goal. *Just head straight to the church. That's all I need to do. Just go straight to the church.*

Once I had somewhat regained myself, I headed right towards the male ward, knowing that was the quickest route. Sidling past the broken entrance, I briefly glanced at the bloody drawing of the Ouija board on the wall, the female patient still nowhere in sight. *Just keep moving. Just keep moving.* I chanted, apprehensively making my way down the hallway. Some of the cell doors were ajar, but I didn't dare take a peek, fearing someone was lurking inside. Then I passed solitary confinement, which echoed with tormented cries. *What's going on- No! Just ignore it! Just head straight to the church for Jack; don't get involved with anyone else!*

Before I reached the gated entrance at the end, I quickly glanced behind me to ensure I hadn't been followed. The corridor was empty, so I shunted the gate, but it didn't budge an inch. *What the?* I tried again and again, but all it did was rattle. *Come on!* I even gave it a few swift kicks, but it still didn't open. *Fuck it! It must be locked!* I couldn't help but seethe. *Why didn't Doctor Hailey give me his keys?!*

With nowhere else to go, I backtracked the way I came. *What way do I go no-*

"Sliiiice, diiiice, did that feel nice?" A ghoulish voice resonated beyond the broken gate, stilling me in my tracks once I was a stone's throw away.

"Haaaack, slaaaash, the blood goes splash." It mimicked something that sounded like a creepy, old nursery rhyme, "Moaaaan, groaaaan, your lips are sewn."

I couldn't bear to listen to them a moment longer, especially when I realised they were gradually getting nearer.

Fuck this! I decidedly backpedalled to solitary confinement, where the harrowing screams still sounded. Much to my relief as well as horror, the gate opened with a groan. The torturous cries of a woman grew louder the further I trudged down the hallway, "**PLEASE STOP!**" They were somewhat deafening even over the siren still whirring.

It wasn't until I reached the side entrance that I clocked three people at the very end: two men and a woman. *What the fuck are they doing?!* The men, who I presumed were inpatients judging by their clothes, were yanking at the nurse's uniform, reminding me of that scene in Cinderella when the ugly sisters were tearing at Cinderella's dress.

"HEY!" I hollered, but the men either didn't hear me or chose to ignore me as they were too preoccupied with what was underneath the dress they had finally managed to rip off. Undeterred, I advanced on them, now able to hear their slimy, carnal voices over the siren.

"Do you know how long it's been since I've had a girl to fuck?" One queried; I wasn't sure who he was talking to until the other replied, "You take one end, and I take the other?"

"PLEASE!" The nurse desperately beseeched, covering herself the best she could with the fragments of dress she still clutched; her undergarments were the only thing preserving her dignity.

"**HEY!**" I hollered again before the men could touch her, "Leave her alone!"

They stilled in their tracks, gazed over their shoulders, and snickered before finally turning to better face me. Only then did I notice they each grasped some sort of weapon. One had a shard of glass, while the other had what appeared to be a jagged piece of metal.

"Maybe we don't want to leave her alone?" The one with the piece of metal jeered.

"What you gonna do if we don't?" The other taunted, bringing up the shard of glass and pointing it threateningly at me.

Knowing they hadn't noticed my gun, judging by their arrogant behaviour, it was now my turn to raise my weapon and intimidate them.

"If you don't leave her alone, I'll blow your fucking brains out." I threatened, and to prove I wasn't joking, I pulled back the hammer with a click.

"Shit! He's got a gun!" The one with the glass panicked, their faces paling in unison.

They couldn't have sidled past me quick enough, disappearing in the direction I would soon be heading.

"Thuh-Thank you!" The nurse stammered, distracting me, "Thank you so much!"

The wind was almost knocked out of me when she unexpectedly pulled me into a fierce hug. Leaning back slightly, I noted her tear-streaked face. *What the hell am I gonna do with her?* I now had someone else to worry about besides myself, and I still had yet to find Jack.

Knowing I couldn't take her with me, I asked, "Do you know where Doctor Kröger's office is?"

When she nodded, I continued, "Head straight there, and you'll find Doctor Hailey."

"Yuh-You're not coming with me?" She asked tremulously.

I shook my head, "No, I've got a friend to find first."

After a little more convincing, the nurse finally left, and I anxiously made my way down the side entrance where those men had disappeared not too long ago. *Hopefully, they've decided not to stick around...* The intersection was just up ahead, and I could no longer hear the continuous thud from the inmate bashing his face against the wall. *Where is he?* I couldn't see him, but there was now a trail of blood that led towards the therapy rooms.

Casting one last glance around to ensure the coast was clear, I turned right, instantly recognising the maintenance room further down. *I just hope this way leads to the church.* Once I reached the end, the only way to go was right, but curiosity got the better of me, and I pressed my ear to the maintenance room door; the sound of sobbing echoed inside. *I guess he isn't getting out anytime soon...* Pushing Doctor Kröger to the back of my mind, I followed the new corridor all the way down until the only way to go was left. *This place is like a maze!* Struggling to create a mental map of the hospital, I felt lost and overwhelmed.

Undismayed, I trudged down the new, much shorter hallway until I reached a T-junction. Peering both ways, I sighed with relief. Nobody was in sight. *But which way do I go?* I decided to head right, figuring the other direction would take me further away from the church.

Then the smell of cooking meat lingered in the atmosphere. *Wait, am I near the kitchen?* I soon spotted the recreation room further down on the left. Keeping my wits about me, I hurried past, vaguely noticing a table laid out with a bottle of wine and candles.

Almost there! I giddily exclaimed, glancing both ways once I came to the end of the corridor. What could only be described as an exorcism on steroids echoed from the female ward, causing my heart to palpitate as panic set in. *No, no, no, I've got to calm down!* I insisted, inhaling several steady breaths. *I'm almost there. I'm almost there.* Once I had composed myself as best I could, I sprinted for the church, hoping it wasn't barricaded and could head straight inside.

Just as the grand-looking, oak double doors were within reach, I stilled when metal suddenly shrieked.

"Doctoooooor Haaaaaaaileeeeeeey..." A deep, otherworldly voice drifted over the siren like a storm on the wind, "Wheeere aaaaare yooou?..."

Fuck, it's him!

Peering over my shoulder just as the groan of a metal gate opened, a shadow slithered along the wall by the entrance to the female ward. *Fuck!* Snapping my attention back upon the church doors, I tried the brass knob, but it wouldn't budge.

FUCK! Then the thud of footsteps infiltrated the atmosphere; I knew I needed to get out of there before being spotted.

Where do I go?! Hurrying back the way I came, it suddenly hit me. *The recreation room!* The cooking smell from earlier returned with a vengeance when I stepped inside, coming to a sudden halt when I saw a patient. *What the?* He was sat at the candlelit table eating what appeared to be thick cuts of meat.

Then I finally recognised him. '***You're looking rather... Tasty today...***'. His hoarse voice came to mind. *What's he doi-*

"Doctooor Haaaaileeeey..." That deep, otherworldly voice emulated nearby, followed by the shriek of metal, "I know you're heeeeere..."

I had no choice but to rush inside, hiding behind the upturned sofa by the stage. *Please don't say anything!* I prayed, my thoughts returning to that strange patient sitting at the candlelit table. ***Please*** *don't say anything!*

The screech of metal abruptly stopped, and I peeked over the sofa to see someone lingering just outside the recreation room door. I couldn't quite make them out due to the dimly lit room and the harsh, red lights still flashing in the corridor, but I could see what could only be described as a massive pair of scissors. *Are those bone shears?!*

To my surprise, the patient sat at the table merely raised their glass of wine to – I presumed – Zed lingering outside, who wandered further down the hallway without a word. *I can't believe it! He didn't say anything!*

Rising to my feet when I was certain Zed had gone, I apprehensively advanced on the strange patient.

"Thanks for that." I said, peering down at him with a forced smile.

Only then did he look at me with his frosty blue eyes, a sanguineous smirk pulling on his craggy face.

"Ah, you're the police officer I've heard so much about..." He commented hoarsely, setting his glass down beside the bottle of Chianti.

News travels fast in here then... I said nothing and turned to leave.

"I'll tell you what." He swiftly piped up, not continuing until I faced him again, "Seeing as I helped you out of a sticky situation, why don't you do me the courtesy of explaining what's on that camera."

At first, I merely stared at him sceptically, refusing to believe he knew anything about it. *How do I even know if we're talking about the same one?*

Folding my arms across my chest, I queried, "What camera?"

"Don't play coy with me," He gruffly retorted, his murderous smirk morphing into something that would put the Cheshire Cat to shame, "I saw you, Aiden, and Jacqueline run off with Doctor Hailey just before this place went into lockdown."

What's that got to do with the camera?

"No patient would willingly leave with two authoritative figures unless it were to benefit them." He tacked on, his frosty blue eyes twinkling triumphantly, "So, I'll ask again, what's on that tiny camera of yours?"

Right then, something dawned on me. *If we're on about the same camera, then how does he know about it?* Only Doctor Hailey and I had seen it. *Until he gave it to Jack...*

"Where is it?" I asked, stepping back to put some distance between us, and he swiftly countered, "That is on a need-to-know basis."

"**Where is it?!**" I demanded once more, my voice hardening in determination.

"And I'm still not telling you." He smugly retorted, clearly aware his evasiveness was triggering something within me.

Oh my fucking God! Why is nothing ever fucking simple?! I just wanted to get out of this hellhole, but yet another obstacle was thrown in my way.

"So, what's on the camera?" He pressured me again, but I just couldn't take it anymore; my muscles quivered as I raised the gun, pointing it at him.

"**TELL ME WHERE THE FUCK IT IS!**" I practically screamed, so angry I couldn't stop my hands from shaking.

His frosty blue eyes slowly shifted to the weapon. The cogs were evidently turning in his head as he mulled over his next course of action.

After a thoughtful moment, he unexpectedly questioned, "Aren't you curious to know **how** I got the camera?" There was no denying the shrewd undertone to his hoarse voice.

Suddenly, I was overwhelmed with such guilt. ***If** he's got the camera, then what about Jack?* I had been so preoccupied with figuring out where the camera was that I had failed to consider what had happened to her.

Lowering the gun, I urged, "Where is she?!"

"She's just in there." He replied without hesitation, gesturing to the service room door.

You've got to be fucking kidding me... I couldn't help but shake my head in frustration.

He must have sensed my annoyance as he suggested, "Why don't you check for yourself?"

Narrowing my eyes suspiciously down at him, I knew this was some kind of trap, but I felt oddly safe knowing I had a gun at the ready.

"Just in there?" I repeated, nodding at the door in question.

"Just in there." He confirmed, his cutthroat smile growing evermore.

I knew not to trust him, but I also needed to find Jack. *How else would he know what the camera looks like if he hasn't got her?* I just hoped I wouldn't find a body, that she was okay, and we could escape unscathed.

Casting the strange patient one last glance, I slowly but steadily advanced on the service room door, which opened with a squeak. Peering inside the windowless room, no one was in sight. *He must mean the kitchen.* I guessed, hurrying towards the door directly opposite.

As I stepped into the commercial kitchen, the stench of cooked meat and fresh gore slapped me in the face, but Jack was still nowhere to be seen. *Where the hell is she?* I quickly scanned the room, noting the counters were splattered with blood as well as offcuts of meat.

"She's just through there." The strange patient unexpectedly spoke up, making me jump out of my skin. Spinning round to face him, I noted he was pointing at the two doors along the back wall. *Something isn't right...* I murmured, keeping my gun poised in fear he would attack me at any given moment.

"You said she's in here!" I retorted, and he repeated while shaking his hand at the doors, "She's just through there."

"**Which** one?" I growled in frustration, peering from the doors back to the patient.

"The left one." He replied condescendingly, as if I should have known the entire time.

Being mindful of keeping him in sight, I made my way sideways towards the left-hand door. *She better be in there.* If not, I had no idea what my next move would be. When I reached the doorway, I glanced over my shoulder at the patient once more.

"She's just through there." He assured me, waving his hand in a shooing gesture and urging me to go inside.

Every fibre of my being was screaming that this was some kind of trap, but I knew I needed to look as I wouldn't forgive myself if I had left Jack behind. *Besides, I still need that camera.*

Holding the gun close, I gingerly opened the door, and a blast of cold air smacked me in the face; the rattle of a fan graced my eardrums. I couldn't make anything out and stepped inside, my shoes thudding against the tiled floor. *God, it's cold in here!* Dabbing my right hand against the matching wall, I found a light switch and immediately flipped it, now realising I was in a walk-in freezer and- *Oh my fucking God!* A handful of bodies were strung up on meat hooks that ran the length of the room, but what horrified me the most was the fact they were human carcasses. Most were stripped of their flesh, but some had been left untouched.

I think I'm gonna be sick! Stifling a gag when the raw, unfiltered scene became too much, I almost turned tail and fled until I heard a muffled cry. *Wait, is someone still alive?!* Shaking off my nausea, I quickly glimpsed at the bodies while apprehensively venturing further inside, soon spotting one that swung from side to side. *Shit! Someone's still is al- Oh my fucking God! Jack!*

"Jack!" I gasped, taking in her face that was twisted in pain.

A wooden peg was wedged in her mouth, pulling her lips so far back they had cracked and bled. Then I clocked the cable ties fastened around her wrists, cutting deep into her skin. *I need to get her down!* Glimpsing at her ankles, they were also restrained.

"I'll get you down!" I vowed, peering back up at Jack's sky-blue eyes.

Holstering the gun into the back of my trousers, I took a look at the hook, unable to stop a grimace from gracing my face.

Shit! A hiss seeped from my lips when I saw the tip had penetrated through the flesh between her shoulder blades. *Fuck that!* Tearing my gaze away, my eyes locked back onto Jack's. *I need to lift her off.* I couldn't even begin to imagine how painful it must be for her. *Then I'll worry about how I'm gonna remove those cable ties.*

"On the count of three, okay?" I asked, beginning the countdown when Jack nodded.

"One." I grasped the tops of her arms.

"Two." I could feel her biceps bunch beneath my fingertips in anticipation.

"Three." I swiftly yanked her upwards off the hook, her harrowing cry muffled against the wooden peg.

Quickly setting Jack down on the white tiled floor, blood dripped down her back with a pitter-patter. *I need to hurry and get her outta here!* As I was about to help her to her feet, I saw fear brimming behind her sky-blue eyes.

"What is it?" I worried, "What's wrong?"

I didn't get the chance to tug the wooden peg out of her mouth before a deep, otherworldly voice delightfully proclaimed, "Found you!"

Just as I snapped my head to stare over my shoulder, a blunt force smacked me across the face, rendering me unconscious.

Chapter Eleven

No one will ever hear my story...

"Waaaakey, waaaaaakeeeeey..." A deep, otherworldly voice resonated around me, but my eyes were too heavy to open. *What... What the?...* My brain felt as if it had been thrown in a mixer and spun until it was nothing but slop, gracing me with the most merciless headache I had ever experienced.
"Waaakey, waaaakeeey..." They persisted, so close their breath tickled my cheek.

A groan reverberated in my throat, not quite reaching my mouth as something sharp and metal was pressed against my throbbing tongue. *What's in my-*
"**I SAID WAKEY FUCKING WAKEY!**" They unexpectedly screamed into my ear, making me jolt awake.

I found myself staring up at a stark white ceiling. *Where am I?!* I tried to sit up, but my wrists and ankles were firmly locked in place, the cuffs fastened to the metal gurney I was lying on. *What the?!* Panicking, I desperately tried to peer around the white-walled room, but my head was also fixed to the stretcher. *WHAT THE FUCK'S GOING ON?!* I wanted to scream for help but couldn't; whatever was stabbing into my tongue also covered my mouth like a muzzle. The contraption was cold and metal, enclosed around my head like a bridle.

I need to get outta here! Not caring how much it hurt, I tried yanking my hands free, but the cuffs were too tight. *Shit, shit, shit! What do I do?!* I couldn't move a muscle to see what was around to analyse the situation. I felt trapped and terrified, knowing this would be my demise if I couldn't escape.

Unexpectedly, a sharp, chiselled face then loomed right in front of me, so close his hot breath beat against my skin. *Who the fuck's he?!* I wondered, staring up at the dark-haired pretty boy who was clad in a bloodstained doctor's coat. *I don't think I've ever seen him before. Which doctor is he?*

With a show-stopping, dazzling smile, he delightfully exclaimed, "Good, you're finally awake!"
He then pulled back to stare longingly down at me with his big, hazel eyes. *Why's he looking at me like that?* I nervously mulled before he came to stand beside me, so close I could see- *What the actual fuck!* I could not divert my gaze quick enough. He wore nothing but that unbuttoned white coat, revealing far more than just his well-defined torso. *Why the fuck isn't he wearing anything else?!*

"I've always liked a man in the services…" He sickeningly began, his eyes never dwindling from mine as he waltzed away, trailing a finger from the top of my trousers all the way down my leg until he reached the cuff.
"I've always wondered what it's like being **inside** one." He wickedly grinned, now standing at the end of the table.
God no! I grimaced, hoping he didn't mean what I thought he meant.

He inhaled a long, deep breath before something hard and metal traced my right leg, distracting me. Straining my eyes to peer down, I couldn't see whatever it was that he had now slipped inside my trouser leg. *What the fuck's he doing?!* **SNIP, SNIP!** The sound of fabric being cut had me freeze. *Is he cutting my trousers?* Cold air now tickled my flesh as he worked higher and higher until I could make out those giant pair of scissors I saw earlier.

It's him! I trembled. *It must be him!* Knowing Doctor Hailey was scared of this man, Zed Stoltzfus, only escalated the fear inside until I could hardly breathe. *But how did he find me?!* My mind raced through all the possibilities until it landed on the moment I was in the walk-in freezer. *He must've been the one who snuck up behind me!*

All speculation vanished when the tip of his blade skimmed around the edge of my briefs, working inwards where I desperately did not want it to go. *He's not gonna-* I gulped. *Cut it off, is he?!*

Zed must have spotted me staring with wide, terrified eyes as he eagerly wondered, "Do you want to watch?"
*'**Watch**'?!* I hawked, my attention snapping up to meet his hopeful gaze. *Watch him do what?!* He then slowly lapped his tongue around his lips in anticipation, biting down on his bottom one, and stared at me for what felt like a lifetime. *I need to get outta here!* And I wriggled against the restraints to no avail.

"How tall are you?" Zed unexpectedly queried, taking me aback.
Why does he want to know my height? He then produced a tape measure from his coat pocket and quickly measured me from head to toe. *What the hell's he doing?!*
A disappointed click of the tongue then sounded from him as he glanced at the measurement, his eyes meeting mine as he uttered, "You're a few inches taller than me..." He then pocketed the tape measure before adding in that creepy tone of his, "Oh well, I guess I'll trim those extra inches off your feet, then you'll fit like a glove."
Wait, what?! Shocked, a sudden coldness expanded within me. *What does he mean '**fit like a glove**'?!*

SNIP, SNIP, SNIP! Zed played with the bone shears with one hand while slipping off my left shoe with the other. *No, no, no!* I panicked, struggling not to let the overwhelming sense of dread consume me. *This isn't happening!* Not knowing what else to do, I waggled my foot from side to side, trying to stop him from grasping my sock. At first, Zed appeared amused, as if he thought it was just a game and I was playing hard to get, but he soon grew frustrated.

"**STAY THE FUCK STILL!**" He ferociously growled, stabbing the pointed end of his shears into my right shin.
An insufferable cry was muffled behind the metal muzzle, my entire body tensing against the pain that gripped me like a vice. Then my tongue involuntarily pulled against the spike, spearing it. *Fuck, that hurts!* It now throbbed in time to my racing heart.
"Now look what you made me do!" Zed barked as the door somewhere by the foot of the gurney opened with a thud.

"What on earth do you think you're doing with **my** patient?!" A hoarse voice bellowed, "And what have you done with your clothes?! Whose coat is that?!"
I thought it was that strange inmate from the recreation room until Doctor Sasin came to stand in my peripheral vision. *What's*

he doing here?! I fretted as the door shut with a click, making me guess it had locked itself.

"Zedekiah?!" Doctor Sasin snapped when Zed, who still lingered by the foot of the bed with the bone shears held skyward, didn't reply.

"I upheld my end of the bargain..." Zed uttered, "I even dealt with that nurse like you asked..."

Meanwhile, Doctor Sasin discarded a tray of instruments on a trolley to my left with a ding.

"So where is **he**?" Zed added, fastening the middle button on his coat, but it did little to hide his member.

Where's who?

"Trust me," Doctor Sasin forebodingly began, "Elon will come looking for him." His glacial blue eyes shifted down to me, chilling me to my core.

Not if he's already dead... I murmured, remembering how badly wounded Doctor Hailey was.

"In the meantime," He continued, directing his attention to Zed, "Why don't you deal with the girl?"

Girl? Then it dawned on me. *JACK!*

A tut echoed from Zed, "If you don't uphold your end of the bargain..." He viciously snapped his bone shears, causing the metal to sing as the blades glided against one another.

I need to get outta here! I need to save Jack before Zed gets his hands on her! But I had no idea how I was going to break free.

"Once you've disposed of her," Doctor Sasin started, wandering over to the door and opening it, "Come back here, and I'm sure you'll have your prize." And by prize, I knew he meant Doctor Hailey.

"If he's not here..." Zed threatened, snapping his shears.

He then left with his massive scissors still held skyward, but I didn't hear the distinct click of the door being shut.

Silence now lingered in the atmosphere before footsteps slowly advanced on me. Doctor Sasin soon appeared beside the trolley with a face dead of all emotion. *What's he gonna do with me?!* I gulped when he began inspecting the instruments littered on the tray, so I wriggled against the cuffs that now felt a little looser.

Holding up what I thought was a pair of pliers, Doctor Sasin reflected, "You know what, Richard, I would've never thought in a million years you were a police officer. You just

don't have that aura about you."
He then deposited the pliers, snatched up a scalpel, and examined it against the light. *Where's he going with this?...*
"Now, paedophile." He continued, pointing the scalpel at me, "Yes. Police officer, most certainly not." He then discarded it with a ding.

"You see, I had a dream." He blissfully continued, "A dream to rid the world of scum, such as paedophiles, serial killers, and rapists, all of whom have an unsound mind. But it's people like you, police officers, lawyers, the government, who believe my ways – my practices – are... Outdated."
Slowly, he inched closer; all the while, his unblinking, glacial eyes were locked onto mine.
"Apparently, it's against the law to physically dig deep into the minds of the insane and figure out what makes them tick." A twisted grin grew on his lips, "But what's the harm if no one knows?"

Just as he was practically nose to nose with me, Doctor Sasin pulled back and said, "So, when I've finished digging deep into my patients' minds, when they're no longer of any use to me, I put them out of their misery."
He then turned for the trolley and plucked up an instrument. I couldn't quite make it out until he plugged it in and turned it on; the metal chatter of a drill rattled through the atmosphere. *No, no, this can't be happening!* I tried to scream for help but accidentally tugged my tongue against the spike; blood now lingered in my mouth.

"Just a scratch." Doctor Sasin wickedly smirked while I fought against the restraints.
He brought the drill down towards my head, but the door opened with a bang, startling us. A slight sneer hooked his upper lip when he gazed over at whoever stood by the door.

"You just missed Zedekiah..." He disdainfully uttered, releasing the trigger on the drill; silence now lingered.

"Pity..." An articulate male voice responded, and I would have jumped for joy if I weren't restrained to the gurney.
Doctor Hailey, he's still alive!

"You do realise you're too late." Doctor Sasin said, "No one's ever going to find out what happened in this hospital once all your living proof has been... Disposed of."

"Do what you wish; I have all the necessary evidence." Doctor

Hailey responded coldly, stunning me.
Wait, what the hell does he mean?!

"I see you haven't changed..." Doctor Sasin commented, a sly smirk pulling at the corner of his lips, "As for your evidence, do you mean **this**?" He buried his hand inside his coat pocket, retrieving the camera.
How the hell did he get that?! Then I realised it was obvious.
Zed... Everything that happened in the recreation room, the kitchen, was all just a set-up...

Doctor Sasin then carefully set the camera down on the trolley, his eyes never dwindling from – I presumed – Doctor Hailey. **SMASH!** With lightning-quick reflexes, Doctor Sasin destroyed the camera with the drill, the remnants scattering around us. He then stood back to admire his handiwork, his devious smile growing triumphantly.

"Am I supposed to be upset?" Doctor Hailey queried flatly, "I've been transferring all the footage for months, so you breaking that camera is only a minor inconvenience."
Based on our conversation the other day in the infirmary, I knew that was true. ***'All the footage has been transferred.'***

"What if I kill your police friend?" Doctor Sasin suggested, gesturing down at me with the drill, and I tensed with dread.
Footsteps then advanced toward us, and I finally saw Doctor Hailey when he came to stand at the foot of the bed.
His dark, penetrating gaze locked onto mine momentarily, shifting to Doctor Sasin when he said, "He's expendable. After all, that's his job."
WHAT?!

Suddenly, the reality of this entire situation was like a slap to the face. *After everything I went through, the sessions, the beatings, all to get his Goddamn footage!* A growl lingered in the back of my throat; I wanted nothing more than to scream.
He doesn't fucking need me, not now he's got what he wants!

"So, what's your big plan then, Elon?" Doctor Sasin wondered, his smile long gone and replaced with his typical detached façade, "Judging by all the effort you've put in, I imagine you want me arrested, yes?"
He didn't give Doctor Hailey a chance to reply before continuing, "And in doing so, I'm sure I'll be questioned regarding all the

footage you've presented them."
Where the hell's he going with this?

Unexpectedly, a cunning smirk spread across Doctor Sasin's face, instantly putting me on edge.
"You may have evidence against me, but you know full well I also have plenty against you." He deviously assured, "I'm certain they'd be eager to hear all about what you did at Blackwater Mental Asylum."
*Wait, what **he** did?* I peered at Doctor Hailey, who looked completely unfazed. *What did he do?* Then I remembered how unwilling he was to tell me. *Did he make up that entire story about Zed?*

"Oh, but that's where you're wrong, Fred." Doctor Hailey retorted, "No one's **ever** going to find out what happened in that hospital."
He then abruptly pulled out a gun from his bloody coat pocket, making Doctor Sasin take an uncertain step back.

"What... What are you going to do with that, Elon?" He fretted, a genuine look of fear gracing his usually apathetic face.

"What I should've done a long time ago." Doctor Hailey callously replied, the click of the hammer resonating all around us.

"Elon," Doctor Sasin calmly began, taking another step back while holding up his hands in a stop gesture, "Why don't we talk about-"

"It was nice knowing you, Fred." Doctor Hailey swiftly intervened before the bang of a bullet whipped through the room; the stench of gunpowder now lingered.
THUD! Doctor Sasin staggered into the lefthand wall; an eerie quietness followed when he collapsed to the floor. *Fuck, fuck, fuck! He's dead! He's fucking dead!*

CLICK! Distracted by the evident sound of a hammer, I stared back at Doctor Hailey, who was now pointing the gun at me. *This is it! I'm gonna die in here!* Fond memories of my family flashed across my mind, but what wrenched my heart was knowing they would never have closure. *Will they think I abandoned them? Left them for someone else?!* That thought alone was more tortuous than anything Doctor Sasin had put me through.

"I'm sorry, Rick." Doctor Hailey apologised, his hold on the gun trembling, "But you know too much."
Too much?! I barely knew anything.
"Don't worry," He began, pressing the barrel to my head, "I'll make it qui-"

"Theeere yooou aaare!" The deep, bloodcurdling voice of Zed sliced across his promise.
A gasp escaped Doctor Hailey when he was forcefully wrenched backwards, causing him to drop the gun with a clatter. When Zed dragged him away, his cries for help faded into the distance until the door shut with a click. That was the last time I ever saw Doctor Hailey.

I need to get out before Zed comes back! Wriggling with all my might, I tried to loosen the cuffs. *Come on! Just a little more!* I tugged and tugged until my right hand popped free. *Yes! Thank God, yes!* Then I practically ripped my other hand out, ignoring the raw sensation left behind by the cuffs.

Now to get the ones off my ankles. I went to sit up but couldn't; the contraption enclosing my face was still fixed to the gurney. *Where's the lock?* Patting the bridle, only smooth metal graced my fingertips. *Where is it?!* I desperately searched the sides, the front, anywhere I could reach, but I still couldn't find the lock. *Where the fuck is it?!*

Then something dawned on me. *What if I can't get this off? Is that how I die? In this room stuck on a table with whatever this fucking thing is on my face?!* Screaming into the muzzle, I grasped the sides of it, yanking and tugging in the hopes it would somehow fall apart. *There must be a lock somewhere!* Giving the contraption another swift jerk, I accidentally pulled my tongue on the spike, my mouth now overpowered with agony that completely consumed my focus. *Gaaah! I just need to get it off!*

Blindly reaching for the instruments on the trolley, I hoped to find the pliers but unintentionally knocked the majority off with a clang. ***NO!*** I raged when I heard the tools scatter across the floor like shrapnel; the only one to survive was the scalpel in my grasp. *Fuck it!* I fumed, wincing when my tongue pulled against the spike. I had never been absorbed by such raw, unchecked suffering before, as if my tongue were ablaze with the constant feeling that it was being ripped in two. *I can't take it anymore!* I needed the spike out now.

Hurriedly sliding the end of the scalpel into my mouth, I wiggled it further and further inside until it touched the foreign object pressed on my tongue. I tried to push the sharp metal off, but it was wedged too firmly in place. *Fuck, fuck, fuck!* Shaking my head in frustration, I instantly regretted it as my tongue felt like it was being torn straight down the middle. *How the hell do I get it off?! What do I do?!* There was only one thing I could think of in my desperation to relieve the pain. *I could cut it off.*

Pulling the scalpel out, I quickly spun it around and wiggled it back inside, the blade slicing the corner of my mouth and making me hiss. *I just hope this works!* But I couldn't ignore the doubt lingering in my gut, knowing the scalpel was too flimsy to cut through metal. *But I've got to try!* I hastily began sawing, my mouth filling with blood whenever I cut myself or the spike stabbed deeper into my tongue. *Come on, come on, please work!* I just wanted the torment to stop.

A distant voice from somewhere outside the room then stilled me, "TRAVIS?!"

I wasn't sure if I had heard it at first, putting it down to my mind playing tricks on me. *It's not real!* I insisted, hacking at the metal spike harder and faster. *They all call me Richard, not Travis!* Blood soon trickled out the corners of my mouth and down my chin. *Fuck this!* ***FUCK THIS!*** I screaked into the muzzle while scrunching my eyes, the pain now unbearable.

Then that voice called again, "TRAVIS?!"

I stopped for a moment to listen, giving myself some much-needed relief.

"WHERE ARE YOU, BUD?!" They hollered, but I quickly focused back on the task at hand.

Not real, not real! I chanted over and over while blood pooled in the back of my throat. It was hard to stop myself from gagging, but I had to as I couldn't handle the agony whenever my tongue pulled against the metal spike.

Then I felt it give. *Have I done it?* It wasn't quite there yet, so I hacked harder and faster, ignoring the excruciating pain.

"TRAVIS?!" They shouted again, the door opening with a groan just as I finally managed to cut it off, dropping the scalpel with a clank.

It's gone! I breathed a sigh of relief, twirling the foreign object around my mouth, but something just didn't feel right.
"Where are you- **WHAT THE FUCK!**" A horrified gasp snapped me back to my senses.

My eyes flew open, but I could hardly make anything out in the dimly lit room. *Where the hell am I?!* It looked like it had once been a therapy room, but now it was an upturned mess. *How the hell did I get here?!* I was crouched on the grimy, tiled floor beside an overturned gurney; a metal trolley lay haphazardly next to it.

"What the fuck have you done, Travis?!" That same voice worriedly piped up; I only now recognised it.
JJ?! And, as if on cue, he came to kneel before me with a leather-bound book tucked under his arm. He looked a little worse for wear, but that was no surprise seeing as he had fallen through the floorboards. *What's he doing here?!*

Confused, I ran my fingers through my hair, which was when I realised the cold, metal contraption was gone. *Wait, what?!* Repeatedly rubbing my face, I wondered. *When did I get rid of it?! **How** did I get rid of it?!* But that thought was short-lived when I scrubbed a hand across my jaw, flinching as the throbbing pain in my mouth returned.

What the fuck's going on?! I panicked when it filled with a tasteless liquid. Spitting it out along with the foreign object, I was baffled by the blood splattered across the tiled floor. *Why can't I taste it?!* Then I spotted something fleshy that looked like a piece of meat. *Wait, is that a tongue?* Then it dawned on me. ***My** tongue?!* I went to trace my tongue around my mouth, but it was no longer in there. *OH MY FUCKING GOD! IT'S MY TONGUE! IT'S MY FUCKING TONGUE!*

"What the fuck did you do?!" JJ disbelievingly queried, turning away to cover his mouth when the sight before him became too much.
I wanted to explain everything but couldn't. *And there's no way I can write everything down.* I debated whether he would believe me; I wasn't even sure what had happened. All I knew was one thing. *No one will ever hear my story...* It would forever remain in this abandoned asylum.

Printed in Great Britain
by Amazon

35784925R00098